Thinking 'Bout Wifin' Her

EVIE SHONTE

ISBN: 1974036790
ISBN-13: 978-1974036790

DEDICATION

This is dedicated to all the women who doubt that love is out there. I promise you there your soulmate is out there. He's just working on being the best him before he steps to you.

CHAPTER ONE

JENAE

I was at Tyson's Corner Mall with my cousin, Tracee, standing at the counter watching the cashier ring up all of the clothes I was purchasing from the H&M when Tracee whispered, "Don't look right now, but the finest nigga I've ever see just walked into the store."

Although I had a boyfriend, I didn't think it would hurt to take a peek, so I turned my head towards the direction of the store's entrance. Lo and behold, the male specimen that walked through the door caused my heart rate to rise.

"Bitch didn't I just say don't look," Tracee asked me as the mystery man locked eyes with me. "See, now he's walking over here."

I gasped and turned around as quick as possible so that I could watch the cashier finish ringing up my items.

"Your total is $386.89," the cashier said with a bright smile on her face.

I was browsing my wallet, looking for the debit card that I wanted to use when I heard someone behind me say, "I got that for you, beautiful."

I turned around and was face to face with Mr. Sexy himself. For a moment, I was unable to speak, but once I got myself together I managed to squeak out, "Nah, that's okay. I can pay for it myself."

"If you insist," he said with his hands in the air as if he surrendered because of my refusal.

I turned back around, having found my Bank of America debit card and swiped it before I took my bag from on top of the counter. I thought that the guy would be long gone by then, but to my surprise, he was waiting for me to finish my transaction. I tried to act like I didn't notice him, but I could feel the corners of my mouth involuntarily turning up into a smile.

"What's your name?" he asked me.

I chortled before I answered. "It's Jenae and yours?"

"My name is Romelo, but you can call me Melo," he answered with a smile on his face, revealing a set of perfect white teeth.

I licked my lips while I looked him up and down, trying to be as subtle as possible. The man was fine as hell. He was lighter than I usually preferred the men I dated, but that wasn't a problem. Romelo was the true definition of a light bright. He had hazel eyes, that were almond shaped, thick, full, and juicy lips, and he sported his hair in a low-cut Cesar. His waves definitely had a sister seasick. And, not to mention he had to be at least 6'4". If I was single I would have been in love with his thick ass, but I wasn't single so I just looked at him before I started for the door.

"Damn you don't have time to stop and talk to me," Romelo asked as he walked behind me.

"I'm sorry, but I have a man, so no. We can't really talk," I said as I turned around to face him, as I walked backward out the door.

"I can respect that. But, her man must not be doing his job if you're here by yourself. If you were mine, I'd always keep you close to me," he said, laying it on thick.

"I just bet you would," I said before I turned back around to walk away. As much as I didn't want to, I ignored Romelo as he called my name while I walked away. I had a situation and I didn't need him causing unwanted drama in my life. That's exactly what a fine ass nigga like him would do too. He looked like he would come in like a tornado, fuck shit up, and then disappear. My boyfriend, Mike, may not have been the recipient of the boyfriend of the year award, but he was consistent and that's what I needed in my life.

"Why you do him like that?" Tracee asked once she'd caught up with me.

I was trying to walk away so fast that I hadn't even noticed that I'd left her behind. "Because... you saw what he looked like. I don't need those kinds of problems in my life."

"Shit, I do. He was fine as hell. I'm sure he had some friends that would be equally as good-looking. You could've at least got his number so that I could meet someone new," Tracee complained.

"Girl, we both know damn well, that you don't need to meet anyone new. Don't you think you have enough niggas calling your phone now, as it is? Didn't you have Derrick hiding in your closet because Black came home?" I asked.

Tracee was a man-eater but she wasn't good at it at all. She had a main dude, Black, but she didn't know how to stay faithful. The chick didn't even know how to keep Black from finding out. The two stayed arguing because she was getting caught up in something new. It was a wonder that Black put up with her, but she was his daughter's mother and she held him down when he was in prison. Still, he was a better person than me, because there was no way I'd be able to put up with that level of disrespect.

"Just because you like to play like the perfect little housewife, doesn't mean that I can. I like to live my life and have fun," was Tracee's response.

"First of all, I'm not a housewife. Second, you wonder why Mike doesn't like for me to hang out with you. This is why," I replied. "Now, did you have any other stores you wanted to go to or can we finally head home?"

"Nah, I'm good. Black's been blowing up my phone anyway. I left him home with Harmony and he claims that he needs to leave the house. Why he won't just take her with him is beyond me."

"Okay, cool," I said as I turned in the direction of the mall's exit, that was closest to where I'd parked my car. My arms were tired from carrying all the bags from my day of shopping. I put them all in the trunk of my Hyundai Sonata before I got in on the driver's side. I wanted to get home and lay down, but I felt crazy since I couldn't get Romelo off my mind.

ROMELO

"Yo, you know shorty?" my cousin Antoine asked.

"Nah. I was just trying to get her number, but she curved me so hard," I responded. I only went into the H&M because I saw Jenae standing at the register. I played myself by calling her name in the middle of the mall like that just for her to keep on walking. Something about her had me stuck, though. She was chocolate as hell, with cocoa butter smooth skin, tall, like a runway model and her eye were so dark and piercing that they almost appeared purple. From outside the door, I could tell that he had an ample ass so it was no wonder she had me confessing my love in the mall.

"Oh, the way you was calling her name, I thought you knew her," Antoine said.

"I know. She said she had a dude, but I'm sure I'll see her again," I said as the two of us walked out the mall. I was only there because I needed something to wear to my little brother's birthday party later that night. I headed back to my house after dripping Antoine off at my club and my girl was sitting on the couch in the same exact spot that I'd left her in.

"Why you smiling so damn hard?" Alyssa asked as

soon as she saw my face.

"Not 'cause of your ass. You ain't move from that spot all day, huh?" I asked as I sat my phone on the table near the front door.

"For what? I didn't have anything to do today and you left me in this house all by myself," Alyssa complained.

"Man, you can go 'head with the bullshit. You act like you not allowed to leave the house without me. Why don't you try going out to look for a job or just chill with your friends instead of trying to be all up under me all the fucking time," I responded.

Alyssa and I had been together for five years. We met when I was away at school at Georgia Tech. I dropped out when my mom got sick and I needed to take care of her and my brothers but Alyssa followed me. Her lazy ass said she was going to transfer to a local school in Baltimore, but she never did. Alyssa moved in with me and stayed up under me all the damn time if she wasn't with my rachet ass cousin.

"You know that I don't have any fucking friends out here," Alyssa yelled. "And, you don't want me hanging around Courtney, so what do you expect me to do?"

"Fuck outta here with that, Alyssa, I said as I headed upstairs because I didn't want to argue with her. What I wanted was for her to go back to Ohio, where she was originally from, but Alyssa insisted on staying just to torture the both of us.

I was getting undressed in my room when I realized that I'd left my phone downstairs on the table, so I threw my t-shirt back over my head and ran downstairs to get it, only to see Alyssa sitting on the couch going through it. "Fuck," I cursed out loud because I didn't want to get into the argument that was obviously coming.

"I don't know why you over there cursing when you're the one cheating on me," Alyssa said before she threw the phone at my head.

I ducked and the phone collided with the wall right where my head originally was. "What the fuck is wrong with you?"

"You think I'm playing with you? You got me stuck in this fucking house, while you out there, fucking other bitches. You ain't shit," Alyssa yelled.

I didn't even have the energy to argue with Alyssa, especially since I had to go and get a new phone. I picked up my iPhone 7 Plus that now had a shattered screen and walked out the house, leaving her there, looking like a fool. I hopped in my Ford F150 and drove to the nearest T-Mobile store to get a new phone. I needed to get rid of Alyssa soon because it was the second time that she'd broken my phone in the past four months. The crazy part was that I wasn't fucking other bitches. Yeah, I got my dick sucked a couple times but I wasn't out in them streets really doing her dirty. Alyssa's antics normally would throw off my entire day, but I wasn't going to let that happen this time.

After getting the new phone, I rushed home because I still needed to get dressed for my little brother, Justin's, birthday party. I couldn't be late to that and I wasn't going to let Alyssa's drama slow me down. When I got back in the house, she was in our bedroom, wrapped in a towel applying lotion to her body with a dress lying on the bed.

"Where you going?" I asked although I wasn't too concerned with her plans.

"To Justin's party, duh," she said as if we were on good terms. She was speaking to me as if I didn't just leave the house to buy a brand-new cell phone.

"No, you not. Who told you that you were even invited?" I asked as I pulled my shirt over my head.

"Quit playing with me, Melo. Justin's like my little brother too. Why wouldn't I be going to his birthday party?"

"Whatever, man. I don't even feel like arguing with you about this tonight," I said before I went into the bathroom so that I could shower. My main goal was to make sure that Justin had a good time and if I had to take Alyssa with me, just to keep the peace, I would do just that.

JENAE

I was sitting on the couch at home, watching Love and Hip Hop Atlanta when the doorbell rang.

"Jenae, get the door!" my mother, Cheryl, yelled from upstairs as if I wasn't going to do it without her urging.

"I'm getting it, ma!" I yelled back as I got up from my comfortable position on the couch. I just knew that whoever was at my door better have had a good reason to be there because I was in for the night; bra off, leggings and bonnet on.

I swung the door open without looking out the window on the door first and was standing face to face with my best friend Sabrina. She had the biggest smile on her face and I just knew that whatever she was going to say, would involve the need for me to put my bra back on. "What's up Bree?" I asked as I moved to the side so that I could let her in the house.

"Bitch, why don't you look happy to see me?" she queried as she stepped over the threshold.

"I am. I'm just tired." I went to take my place back on the couch. "What's up? Why you all dressed up?"

"Because there's a party tonight and I wanted you to come with me," Sabrina answered. "So, don't take a seat on the damn sofa 'cause we need to go upstairs to pick out a good outfit for you to wear."

"What makes you think that I want to go to a party, on a Wednesday night, at that. I've got work in the morning."

"You can call out of work once in your life. You're always either u under Mike's wack ass or at work. Have a little fun, please. Besides, I want you to meet the guy that I'm talking to."

I let out a sigh before I stood back up. "Okay, but I'm not staying late. And he better be cute."

"He is. I promise, you'll like him and we'll have fun," Sabrina said trying her best to get me to agree to go out.

"I said I'd go, but if I don't have any fun you owe me one, bitch."

"Best friend, you know I wouldn't steer you wrong," Sabrina said assuring me.

I took a quick shower and got dressed in the outfit that Sabrina picked out for me, which was a pair of high-waisted black pants, that laced up each leg and a cropped AC/DC concert tee. I wanted to wear a pair of black and white Vans, but Sabrina insisted that I wear a pair of black t-strap sandals and after only a half hour I was ready to leave the house. We got into Sabrina's white Nissan Altima and headed towards Power Nightclub, where the party would be taking place. I didn't want Mike to wonder where I was so, I shot him a text to let him know that I was out with Sabrina.

She saw me with my phone in my hand and said, "I know you not texting your bitch made boyfriend."

I looked at her and sucked my teeth. "Mike isn't a bitch. Just because you don't like him, doesn't mean that he doesn't treat me good."

"Whatever! You and I both know that he's the true definition of a fuckboy. Which is why I'm taking you to this party tonight, so that you can meet someone new. Justin has two brothers and they're all fine as fuck, too." Sabrina couldn't stand Mike because eight months ago, while he and I were on a date, he got robbed. Mike gave the kid who robbed us everything, including the promise ring that I was wearing. I didn't see things the same way as Sabrina because I was just happy to be alive. Either way, ever since then, she was trying her hardest to set me up with someone new.

"Sabrina, stop. No nigga is going to make me want to breakup with Mike. You've been trying for so long and it hasn't worked yet," I said although I knew that it fell on deaf ears. Sabrina wouldn't give up until I was no longer with Mike.

There was a line at the door that went all the way up the street. I hated waiting in long lines to get in the club. I never would make a fuss about it. I just rarely went out because of it. However, Sabrina grabbed my hand and led me straight to the front door. "Hey, we're on the list," she said to the big burly bouncer.

"Nah, you not 'cause we don't have no list," he said trying to shoo us away and to the end of the line.

I was fully prepared to turn around and wait at the back of the line because I didn't want to be embarrassed trying to get in the club for free only to be turned away, but Sabrina wasn't going for it. "Okay, so if you don't have the list, then who does because Justin told me that I would be on the list?"

"Man, stand over there and I'll find out," the bouncer said. He clearly didn't want to deal with us, when the line was already long as hell and it wasn't even eleven o'clock.

We stood over to the side but the bouncer helped another patron. He had no intentions of finding someone with the list. Once again, I tried to walk to the end of the line, since the bouncer clearly had no plans to help us, but Sabrina stopped me. She had her phone up on her ear with a determined look on her face. "Yeah, Justin, I'm outside with my girlfriend and this baldheaded black motherfucker is telling me that there's no list. Can you come get us, please?... Okay, thank you."

I folded my arms across my chest as I waited. We were garnering stares from the girls in the line and it bothered me because I hated to be the source of conversation and that's exactly what we were. It took about five minutes for a guy to emerge from inside the club and speak to the bouncer that denied us entry. "Y'all two, come on," the bouncer said as he pointed at us.

Sabrina showed him her ID after he looked at mine. She couldn't just go inside without saying something petty to him. "Thank you for finding that list for us."

The guy laughed at her but didn't say anything. When we got inside, at the front there was a girl collecting the money for the cover charge, but the guy that told the bouncer to let us in was also waiting on us so that we didn't have to pay.

Sabrina walked over to him and gave him a hug. He hugged her so tight that he lifted her feet up off the ground. They shared a peck on the lips before Sabrina finally turned to me and said, "Jenae, this is

Justin. Justin, this is my best friend in the whole world, Jenae."

"Nice to meet you," I said to him with a smile. He just nodded at me before he led us inside and upstairs to his VIP section.

CHAPTER TWO

ROMELO

My eyes locked on Jenae the moment that I saw her walk into the VIP section with my little brother, Justin's, new girlfriend. I wanted to walk over to her and say something, but Alyssa was sitting next to me and would blow up my spot if I attempted to say anything to another girl. When Jenae looked over at me, I looked away. I didn't want Jenae to see me sitting with Alyssa. I didn't want to hurt my chances of getting with her, eventually.

I found my eyes on her again when she went to sit at one of the tables with her friend. "Yo, Alyssa, I'll be right back. I'm going to go and talk to Justin."

"Okay, babe," Alyssa said surprising me but when I saw her phone in her hand with Snapchat up, I knew that she wouldn't care about anything I did. That dog filter was going to hold her attention for at least the next fifteen minutes or so.

I walked up to Justin and gave him dap before I waited to be introduced to the ladies he was sitting with.

"Melo, you remember my girl Sabrina and this is her friend ummm…"

"Jenae," I said finishing his sentence for him.

Jenae, who was paying me no mind when I walked up, looked up from her phone and into my eyes. I felt a spark and I was sure that she did as well, but she tried to pretend that she didn't by rolling her eyes and saying, "Oh, it's you again."

"Yeah, it's me again. When are you gonna let me take you out?" I asked.

"I bet the girl that you're here with wouldn't like that and neither would my boyfriend," she said before she looked back down at her phone shutting me down for the second time in just one day.

"Damn," Justin said at the end of our exchange. Your friend is cold," he said to Sabrina.

"It's cool," I said trying to play it off. "You

having a good time, bro? You need anything?" I quizzed.

"Nah. I'm straight now that my lady is here. Thank you for putting this together for me."

"No problem. I'm going to go back over to Alyssa before she starts tripping. It was nice seeing you again, Sabrina," I said.

"And it wasn't nice seeing me?" Jenae asked.

"It was good seeing you too, but I'll see you again, Jenae," I replied before I licked my lips. I knew that I would certainly see Jenae again and I wasn't going to stop trying to get to know her until she was mine.

"When I got back to Alyssa, I poured some Hennessey into my cup and refilled hers as well. "Here."

"What's this?" she asked before she took a small sip.

"It's the Henny, right there. You almost ready to go?" I asked because I wasn't feeling the party anymore. My other brother had arrived and he'd make sure that Justin had a good time.

"Uh, no. We just got here. I don't even have a buzz yet. Who are those girls over there with Justin?" Alyssa asked after the took the rest of the Hennessey down in one swallow.

"That's Justin's girl and her friend," I said and my eyes locked on Jenae's from across the large section. I smiled at her and she looked away but not before I saw a smile rise on the corners of her mouth.

I tried to make the best of an awkward situation since Alyssa didn't want to leave. I partied with my brothers and stayed on my best behavior by not dancing with any of the females presents. I just didn't want Alyssa to have another reason to fly off the handle.

When I got home that night, I thought that we'd be able to go to bed without an argument, but Alyssa was drunk as hell and couldn't help but start one.

"Man, get off my damn belt," I said as Alyssa tried to undo my belt to get me to have sex with her.

Alyssa was down on her knees looking up at me when she spoke. "Are you turning down head, right now?"

"Yeah. You drunk as shit. I don't want any drunk pussy. Plus, I gotta make a run," I said as I pushed her away causing her to fall onto her butt in front of me.

Alyssa hopped to her feet and mugged the shit out of me. "Are you serious right now? What bitch you 'bout to run out of this house to go fuck?"

"Man go 'head with the bullshit. I gotta go run something to Keraun. You always think that I'm fuckin' a bitch. If I do, will that make you move back home?" I asked.

I watched as the tears welled up in her eyes. After seeing her cry so many times in the past for the smallest of reasons, I wasn't fazed. "You really want me to move back home? My whole life is here."

"Is it really?" I asked. "You were just complaining that I'm always leaving you and you have nothing to do, so what life do you have here?"

"You know what the fuck I mean, Melo. You're my life and you're here," she said as the tears were streaming down her face.

"That's the issue. I can't be your entire life. You have to have more to live for because instead, you're just nagging me. I'd help you get on your feet, whether it's here or in Cincinnati, but I can't live with you anymore, shorty."

"So, that's it? You don't want to be with me anymore?" she asked wiping the tears away, no longer looking sad, but pissed off.

"You telling me that you still want to be with me? You think I'm cheating. You're unhappy. Why you want to stay? Just to say that you have a man?" I asked speaking the truth.

"Are you cheating?" Alyssa asked, folding her arms over her chest.

"What? No, I'm not cheating. I don't want to cheat on you which is why I'd rather end this, now."

"See, because I find it funny that you suddenly want to break up out of nowhere. Like, this has to be coming from somewhere. You got a side chick that's asking you to leave me?"

I wiped my hand down my face because this bitch was crazy. "Fuck this shit. I'm out. I'll give you a few days to move out, but I'm serious about wanting you out the house, so you better start looking for a place or plane tickets."

"Fuck you," Alyssa yelled as I walked out the house.

JENAE

After the party, Sabrina dropped me back off at home. I was more than ready to go to bed, but first I had to take a shower and wipe off my makeup. I wiped the makeup off first and then I hopped in the shower. All the while, Romelo was on my mind. I let the water beat on my body and imagined his hands caressing me. I was in a trance and didn't notice that I was using my own hands to touch my body. My fingers found my swollen clit and rubbed it in a circle, while I had my eyes closed, envisioning Romelo's face. As soon as I came on my own fingers, my eyes popped open with the realization of what I'd done.

I loved Mike, but Romelo was on my mind heavily and I didn't even know him. I didn't know what to do because it was clear that I'd be seeing him again. I wasn't sure if I'd be able to resist another one of his advances.

The next morning Mike was calling my phone, bright and early. I sat up in the bed and answered the phone. "Hello," I said with a frog still in my throat.

"You want to go and get some breakfast?" he asked.

"Umm, okay, I guess so," I replied.

My cousin Tracee, who owned a salon and was my boss, had already texted me saying that she didn't need me to come into work for the day because she had to take Harmony to the doctor's office so I was off.

"Cool, I'm outside your house," Mike said and sucked my teeth.

"Alright. Give me like fifteen minutes and I'll be out." I hung up and got out of bed, although it was hard because I was exhausted. I hated when Mike showed up at my house without calling first. It only bothered me because if I did the same thing, he'd have no problem cursing me out. That was something that I found out the hard way, unfortunately. It made me think that he was cheating on me but Mike assured me that it was all in my head. Either way, I kept my ear to the street and never heard anything about him being with other chicks.

It was the spring, therefore, it was a t-shirt and jeans type of day. My t-shirt had a deep v-neck and I had on a pair of distressed boyfriend jeans. I decided to wear my black and white Vans that Sabrina would let me wear the night before. I took my scarf off and let my wrap fall into place. I didn't bother with any makeup because Mike would be pissed if I took longer than fifteen minutes. I grabbed my black varsity jacket off the coat rack on my way out the door.

"You went out last night?" Mike asked as soon as I got in the car.

"Yeah, Sabrina made me go with her to her boyfriend's birthday party. It was last minute," I replied.

"Why you ain't call me to tell me you were headed out, though? People told me that some nigga was all up in your face, all night," Mike said catching me by surprise.

"Huh?" I was absolutely thrown off. Mike was never the jealous type so I wasn't sure where it all was coming from.

"What nigga at the club that you went to was all up in your face?" Mike asked again.

"Wasn't no nigga in my face. Like, I said the first time, I was at the party because of Bree's boyfriend's birthday party. I was introduced to his brother but after the nigga said hello he walked away. Where are you getting your information from?" I quizzed.

"Don't worry about that, just know that when you out in these streets, I got eyes on you," Mike replied, refusing to answer my question.

"Mike, you're tripping, right now. It was very last minute that I even went to the party. I stayed for like an hour before I went home. Is this why you came to my house this morning to take me out because you really wanted to question me about last night?"

"Nah, I wanted to see you," he said as he rubbed my thigh. Clearly, he was thinking that would make me feel better, but clearly, he was wrong.

I wanted to push his hand away, but I wasn't that petty. I let him rub on me while I had my arms folded across my chest. I went to Denny's for breakfast and the entire mean I was giving him the silent treatment. It wasn't as if he was engaging me in any conversation either since he was on his phone the entire time.

The food was good and I ate it faster than Mike could finish his breakfast, so my eyes were wandering around the restaurant when in walked the girl that was with Romelo at the club the night before. My eyes locked on hers and before I could look away, the trick hit me with the stank face. I couldn't do anything but chuckle before I actually looked away.

The girl didn't know me but it was obvious that she didn't like me. When Mike was ready to leave, I was more than ready to go, myself. The girl was still standing near the door, waiting on a table as Mike and I walked up to the front so that he could pay. I was too busy minding my business to notice that she was even stepping to me.

"Excuse me," I heard a voice say from behind me

as well as felt a tap on the shoulder.

I turned around and was face to face with Romelo's date. "Yes?" I asked confused as to what the girl could possibly want.

"How do you know my man?" she quizzed.

I was dumbfounded because the trick had the nerve to ask me that question, but I decided to play dumb. "Ummm, who is your man?"

"Romelo. You were talking to him last night at the club. I also saw the two of y'all staring at each other, making googly eyes and shit," she clarified.

"Oh, I don't really know him, other than the fact that his brother is my best friend's boyfriend." I patted her on the shoulder before saying, "You have nothing to worry about. I can promise you that." I then turned back around to stand shoulder to shoulder with Mike.

Mike was busy giving me the side eye, while he paid the hostess for our meal, but he didn't speak on what just took place. I knew that once I got in the car, I would be hearing an earful, though. Romelo was getting me into all kinds of trouble and all I'd done was turn the dude down, twice. I couldn't help but imagine what would happened if I gave in to him.

In the car, Mike said, "Who was that?"

"I don't know. Some girl that was at the club I went to yesterday."

"But you know her dude? Was that the same nigga that I was asking you about earlier?"

I sucked my teeth before I answered. "Yes, but like I said earlier, I wasn't all up in the nigga's face. I went to the club last night with Sabrina and met her new boyfriend. His brother came over and introduced himself to us, then he went back over to the girl you just saw. Obviously, he has a girl, meaning I wasn't all up on him." I didn't like the idea of explaining myself over and over again, especially when I didn't feel like I'd done anything wrong.

"Man, I'm taking you home. You want to be all up in some nigga's face, then give him a call," Mike said.

I knew he wanted me to object. I knew that he wanted me to tell him that I was sorry, but I didn't do a single thing wrong, therefore I wasn't kissing his ass at all. "That's cool."

Mike cut his eyes at me but didn't say anything else. He just took me home. When I got there my mom and little sister were sitting on the couch watching Bad Girls Club. "Reality TV rots your brain," I said when I walked through the door.

"Who the fuck pissed in your orange juice this

morning?" my mom asked with her face twisted at my comment.

"I'm sorry, I just got into it with Mike because someone told him that I was in some other dude's face last night, while I was out at the club," I said before I took a seat on the loveseat.

"Why do you even deal with him?" my little sister Leilani asked.

It seemed like I was the only person who actually liked Mike and at that moment I was beginning to ask myself that very same question. "I don't even know right now," I admitted.

My mom, never the one to bite her tongue, laughed at my response. "You finally starting to see where I've been coming from."

"I guess. He just really pissed me off. Like, I've never cheated on him and I've had the opportunity to, but the fact that he wouldn't take my word for it was the crazy part," I explained.

ROMELO

I stayed at my cousin, Antoine's house since going home wasn't an option, as long as Alyssa was still at my house. I cursed myself for not leaving with any of my clothes, but when I got up, I just rushed downtown and got something to wear. I was in Urban Outfitters when I ran into Sabrina, Justin's girlfriend.

"Hey, it's Melo, right?" she asked me with a friendly smile on her face. Sabrina was bad as hell. A part of me wondered how Justin pulled her because he wasn't her type. I didn't know Sabrina but I'd heard about her and she was popular on Instagram. She mainly dated hustlers and Justin was as square as they come.

"Yeah, you work here?" I asked because she was folding shirts on a table.

"No, I just like folding shit," she joked, causing me to chuckle. "But yeah, I'm an assistant manager here. Did you need any help finding anything?"

"Nah. I just came to get some draws," I replied ready to walk off when I thought about her friend. "Wait, as a matter of fact, I do need something. Let me get your homegirl's phone number."

She looked at me with her eyes bugged out her head. "Who, Jenae?"

I wanted to tell her that was a dumb ass question since that was the only friend of her that I knew but I didn't since I wanted information from her. "Yeah, her."

"She got a boyfriend and from what I hear you got a girl, so no," Sabrina said point blank.

"Man, you joking, right? I don't have a girl and I don't give two fucks about some wack ass nigga. Just give me her number and I'll handle the rest," I said hoping that Sabrina would do what I wanted her to do.

"Nope. What kind of friend would I be to do that?" Sabrina asked with her hand on her hip.

I knew she was serious about not giving me Jenae's number so I decided to drop it. "Where yall keep y'all draws at?"

"They're upstairs in the men's department. If you need anything, just let me know."

"Yeah, alright," I said as I walked away. I wanted to avoid sounding as salty as I felt. I just knew that Sabrina would give me the number no questions asked. I wasn't used to not getting my way. On my way out the door, Sabrina waved at me but I didn't bother saying bye back because I wanted that phone number that she refused to give.

I was headed to meet with Keraun when Alyssa called my phone. I wanted to ignore it, but curiosity got the best of me and I answered it. "Hello?"

"I ran into your little girlfriend from the club last

night," Alyssa said sounding bitter but I was confused.

"What the fuck are you talking about?" I queried.

"That bitch who's face you were all up in, last night at Justin's party. She was at Denny's with some nigga. You leaving me for a bitch that don't even give a fuck about you," Alyssa quizzed.

"Man, go the fuck ahead with the bullshit, Alyssa. I told you that I wasn't fucking with any other bitch last night. What do you need so that you can get on your feet and out of my fucking life? You need money? You need me to buy you a plane ticket? What?" I asked, dead serious. I would give her whatever she needed if it would get her to leave me alone.

"Can you just come home so that we can talk about this?" Alyssa asked in a soft tone.

"I'll come by there, but it won't be to get back together. I'm coming to give you money and that's it," I replied.

"Okay, how long until you're here?" Alyssa asked.

"I've got some business to take care of. I'll call you when I'm on my way," I said before I hung up the phone.

I drove straight to Keraun's place and went in my

trunk to get out a duffel bag. Before I could knock on the door, he was answering it. "What up, nigga?" Keraun said as he gave me dap.

"Ain't shit. This your cut of the money from that deal last week." I handed him the duffel bag. Keraun put me on to a new customer and the money was his finder's fee. It wasn't something that I did often, but when Keraun looked out the way he did, it was nothing to offer him a cut.

"Man, you know I don't need this shit," he said as he took the bag.

"But you taking it, ain't you?" I said laughing.

"You know I ain't gonna turn it down. Not when I just found out that I got twins on the way." Keraun stepped to the side so that I could walk in the house. He already had NBA2K loading on the TV since he knew that I was on my way over.

"Twins, nigga?" I asked.

"Yeah, fucking Paris called me the other day telling me that she was pregnant. I ain't believe it at first, but she facetimed me when she was at the doctor's office yesterday and I heard two heartbeats. Shit fucked me up," Keraun said taking a seat on the couch and picking up one of the controllers.

"Damn. They yours?" I quizzed because Keraun

and Paris were no longer together.

"That's what she saying. We'll see when they get there. Those twins will make five kids for me. That's a fucking basketball team," Keraun joked.

"You the nigga that keep fucking Paris ass raw. You know she get pregnant just by you looking at her. I thought you stopped dealing with her crazy ass, anyway."

Keraun sighed before saying, "I did, but I went over to her house to give her money for the kids and slipped up. Now, I gotta tell Leilani that I slipped up with Paris. Shit's all fucked up, bro."

I couldn't help but laugh because Keraun always puts himself in fucked up situations. "Nigga, you know Lani gonna bounce on you, damn."

"I know man, fuck."

CHAPTER THREE

SABRINA

"Girl, that nigga was just here looking for you," I told Jenae while we were at Chipotle. She met me for lunch to tell me about Mike.

Jenae scrunched up her face as if I'd just said something disgusting. "What you mean he was looking for me. How the fuck did he even know you worked at Urban?"

"Okay, well he didn't come here looking for you. He was here shopping and when he saw me he asked for your number. I knew your ass would curse me out if I gave it to him, but I was hella tempted," I explained. Romelo was sexy as hell and I felt like he'd treat my best friend a hell of a lot better than Mike. The only drawback was his girlfriend.

"Oh, 'cause you had me thinking the nigga was a real life stalker. But, if you see him again, you can give him my number," Jenae said surprising me.

"Nae, you sure? I mean you did just say that his girl approached you when you were in Denny's. You don't want that type of drama in your life," I said. While I thought it would be fun to potentially go on double dates with Jenae, I wanted to make sure that she knew what she was getting involved in.

"I have a dude, he has a girl, meaning that whatever happens between us would just be fun." Jenae threw up her hands in a nonchalant gesture. "Truthfully, that nigga is thick as hell. I just want to see what it looks like."

"What, what looks like?" I asked because I was lost.

"The dick, duh. I just imagine that it's like a Mandingo," she admitted before opening her mouth and laughing.

"You so nasty," I replied. "But if he's anything like his brother, I'm sure that it will be."

Jenae put up her hand and said, "Okay," before I gave her a high five.

"What are you doing when you get off?" Jenae

asked as she started to clean up the lunch in front of her.

"I'm supposed to chill with Justin, why? Did you want to do something?"

"No." She waved me off. "Go have fun with your boyfriend. I wanted to go to the movies, but I'll just call Leilani to see if she wants to go."

"All right. Thank you for coming down here. I'll call you later. I gotta get back to work." I gave Jenae air kisses before I put the rest of my burrito in the bag and headed back to Urban Outfitters to finish my shift.

Just like he'd promised, Justin was parked right outside of the store when I got off. I got in his car and gave him a kiss on the lips. "Hey, thank you for picking me up. I hate driving down here and trying to find parking."

"You know I got you, right? How was work?" Justin asked as he pulled out into traffic.

"It was okay. Your brother stopped by," I said because I wanted to get whatever information he was willing to give me about his brother.

"Who? Melo?" Justin asked.

"Yeah, Romelo. He was trying to get me to give him Jenae's phone number," I replied.

"Oh, he ain't gonna stop until she's his, just so you know," Justin explained and I'd already gotten that vibe from him.

"Your brother has a girlfriend," I said. I didn't like the way that Justin was okay with my friend being a side chick.

"He don't fuck with Alyssa like that. Yeah, she there but he don't take her out or anything. I was surprised to see her at the party last night," Justin said like that was supposed to make things better. Romelo still had a girlfriend and that was all that mattered in my eyes.

"But he has a girlfriend," I said repeating myself.

"Yeah, All I'm saying is that I don't know how long that relationship will last," Justin responded.

"I'm not going to argue with you about this, Justin. What are we about to do?"

"No one was arguing. That's you getting upset with something that don't even have anything to do with us," Justin said and he had a point. I wasn't playing the side chick and as far as I knew he didn't have one. "You hungry? I want to get something to eat?"

I shrugged. "I can eat if you're treating."

Justin laughed at me. "Yo, my aunt used to always

say that when in doubt, feed your girl and she'll be happy."

"Well, she was right. You can always make me feel better if you feed me, preferably some wings. Please, and thank you." I was grinning from ear to ear and when we got to the red light, Justin gave me a kiss on the lips.

Justin was nothing like any of the other guys I'd ever dated. For starters, he was younger than me although it was only by a year. However, growing up I only dated older guys and at twenty-four, I was used to dating men thirty and up. But, Justin had his shit together. He graduated from Temple University with a degree in finance. He had a job lined up and looked good as hell on paper. Plus, he could dress his ass off. My man was a real catch. I just had to get used to the fact that he wasn't the typical drug dealer and didn't have money coming in from all directions. Yet, that was something that I could live with since I wouldn't be worried if the FEDs were watching like I'd done in all of my previous relationships.

Justin took me to a sports bar down the street from his apartment complex, where we had drinks and ate, but mainly he watched the basketball game. Since he wasn't paying me any mind, I was engrossed in my Instagram. I posted a few pictures of myself and the food. I wasn't surprised when I received a DM from my ex-boyfriend Cisco. I rolled my eyes up into my head when I read the message:

You went and found yourself a new nigga, huh?

I left the DM on read and didn't bother to respond. Why would I do something like that, though, because Cisco sent me another message:

You know I can see that you read it, right?

That got a response out of me:

I sure can, but I don't care. Get out of my DMs, nigga.

Cisco broke my heart nine months prior but if you asked him, he did nothing wrong. I'd like to think that the constant baby mama drama from a baby that he had while we were together would be enough to break my heart. However, it was the slit tires on my car from the trifling bitch that put the icing on the cake. A day didn't go by that Cisco wasn't trying to find his way back in, but I knew better. I'd learned from my mistakes and I knew that I deserved better. No amount of money was going to make me stay with someone that didn't love me the way that I deserved to be loved.

"You okay?" Justin asked as he rubbed me on my thigh.

I didn't even realize that I was frowning until he checked to see if I was fine. "Yeah. I'm fine. I'm just tired. I have to open the store tomorrow. Do you think you can take me home?"

"Yeah. You sure you okay, though?" Justin asked again as he waved over the waitress.

"I'm sure," I lied. Although I didn't want it to happen, Cisco was suddenly consuming my thoughts and I didn't feel comfortable with that. I was in a daze from the moment that Justin and I left the restaurant and I got home and into my bed. Justin tried to spend the night but I needed to be alone. I had to resist the urge to call Cisco and tell him how I was feeling, but I managed to with the help of a large glass of wine and a bowl of loud.

JENAE

It had been a few days since I'd seen Mike. He was still upset with me about what people were saying about me being up in Romelo's face. I wasn't about to kiss Mike's ass, so I went about my life as usual. I loved Mike but I hated a lot of his ways and his jealousy is what bothered me the most.

I had to head to work at my cousin's hair salon as her assistant, meaning I was up hella early and needed coffee in my life. I stopped at the Dunkin Donuts, near the salon. I was staring up at the menu, trying to select what I wanted when I heard someone whisper in my ear. "You look beautiful, today."

I turned around and realized that I was face to face with Romelo. I blushed, although I didn't want to. "Thank you. You're handsome as well."

Romelo's light skin turned red at the compliment, but he tried to play it off. "I just knew that I was going to have to stalk you, just to be able to see you again, but here you are."

"But, you did resort to stalking, didn't you? You were at my friend Sabrina's job a few days ago trying to get my phone number, weren't you?" I said blowing up his spot.

He put his hand over his mouth while he laughed before he grabbed his huge beard and spoke. "Yeah, you right. I tried to get your number but she wouldn't give it to me. I'm hoping I can get it now, though."

"Wouldn't your girl have a problem with that?" I asked knowing damn well I didn't care about whatever girlfriend he had. I was attracted to Romelo, I couldn't deny that. Now with me and Mike on the outs, it felt like it was the perfect chance to explore what else was out there.

"Ma, I'm single," he said and I looked into his eyes before I broke into an involuntary fit of laughter.

"Now, why you lying? I saw your girl at the party. She also approached me while I was with my boyfriend in Denny's. Messed up my whole situation and everything," I said.

Romelo let out a deep laugh. "I'm serious. I'm single. I let her go on her own way because it wasn't working out. I would say that I'm sorry she messed up your situation, but I'm not because it'll give me a chance to get your number."

"You must be used to getting your way," I said walking around him so that I could go pay for my latte.

I knew that he would follow me and he did just that. "I am, but I just want to get to know you.

Nothing more than friends."

"Just friends, huh?" I asked with an eyebrow raised. I didn't fully trust his words.

"Yeah, just friends, until you're ready to make a change."

I looked at him and thought long and hard before I said, "Okay, I'll give you my phone number."

Romelo pulled out his phone and said, "Now was that so hard?"

"Boy, you better take this number before I change my mind."

After running into Romelo in the Dunkin' Donuts, I walked into Tracee's salon with a smile on my face. There weren't any customers in there yet so I took a seat at one of the dryers in the back and pulled out my phone so I could tell Sabrina the news. Tracee was sitting on the stood behind her salon chair, staring over at me with a smirk on her face. As soon as I noticed her looking I said, "What?"

"What's got you smiling so damn hard? You got some last night?"

"No. I'm not even talking to Mike, right now. I ran into that guy from the mall at the Dunkin Donuts. I gave him my number too," I admitted.

"Good, 'cause that nigga was sexy as hell and if you didn't want to get on it, I sure would have. What's going on with you and Mike though? Y'all broke up?"

I shrugged. "We didn't break up officially, but that's where we're headed. I'm just not feeling it anymore."

"Good, 'cause I never really liked him anyway," Tracee admitted.

"I know, Tracee. Nobody likes him."

"I'm just saying that dude from the mall was sexy as hell and he looked like he had money," Tracee said revealing the real reason that she wanted me to get with Romelo.

"Mike has money. Money isn't the reason that I like him. Right now, I'll admit, I just like the attention that he's giving me. But, the ball is in his court. He still has to call me."

"You know that nigga is definitely going to be calling you. After he was yelling your name like that in the mall when you turned him down, I'm sure that nigga will be calling you in the next hour or so," Tracee said.

I laughed at the memory. That was part of the reason I have Romelo my number. Clearly, when the man saw something he wanted he went after it and that was a hell of a turn on for me.

After lounging around for thirty minutes, Tracee's first client, Brenda finally arrived after being twenty minutes late. I got my day started because Tracee was all booked up and the faster that I got them prepped the faster I'd be able to get out of the salon.

I worked for her only because she offered the job. I went to school at Barry University in Miami, but after a year, I realized that it just wasn't for me. The problem was, I didn't know what I wanted to do and Tracee offered me the job as her assistant while I found myself. That was five years ago and I was content with my position in life, although my mother tried to get me to figure things out. I never did because I was enjoying my twenties.

At the end of the day, Tracee still had three people she had to finish, but I'd cleaned up and prepped everyone so I was out the door by 4:30 and had a pocket full of tips. I was walking to my car when I noticed Mike leaning against it. I wanted to turn around and go back to the salon. The last thing that I wanted to deal with was him. I was about to do just that when Mike started walking towards me. "Wait, Jenae, I just want to talk."

"Well, I don't," I responded.

"Look, I'm sorry. You don't have to forgive me, but I wanted you to know that I didn't mean to blow up on you like that. I was just hearing shit in the streets about the cat Romelo and I felt like he was trying to be smart by talking to you," Mike said, peaking my interest.

"He knew who I was already and that the two of us were together?" I asked. I didn't take Romelo to be that kind of guy, but I didn't know him well enough to know for sure.

"Yeah. We been beefing for a few months now and…" Mike looked up and to the left, something he did when he was lying before he continued. "He knew you were my girl when he met you in the club. I shouldn't have overreacted like that."

I pursed my lips while I decided that I wanted to say. "Thank you for apologizing, Mike, but at the same time, you blew up on me for no reason and I didn't like that. I've overlooked a lot of shit when it comes to you and truthfully, I'm tired."

"So, what does that mean?" Mike asked for clarification.

"It means that I'm done. I can't do this anymore. I love you, but my feelings aren't the same as they used to be. I know you feel the same way."

Mike nodded his head while he laughed. "You got

it, Nae. You can break up with me if you want to, but just know that there isn't another nigga out there like me."

"Don't do all of that, Mike," I said trying to stay calm while he was trying to cause a scene.

"You must already be fucking that nigga then if you so okay with breaking up with me."

I didn't dignify that with a response. I just walked away and went to the passenger side of my car. I left Mike to argue on the street with himself because I wasn't the one.

ROMELO

I felt good after getting shorty's number and even better that it was her choice to give it to me and that I didn't get it from her homegirl. Once I secured the number I felt good about starting my day. I ran into Jenae when I was leaving the house of some chick I'd met in the pool hall the night before. Weed, liquor and good head had me accidentally spending the night with the chick and I woke up with a hangover so I stopped by Dunkin Donuts to get a black coffee. I just happened to see Jenae there and it felt like it was fate or some shit like that, that had me constantly running into the chick.

After leaving Dunkin' Donuts I had to stop off at my house so that I could grab some clothes. I was buying new things every time I needed to change my clothes, plus Alyssa should have made her way out of my house. When I got there, I checked every room and was happy as hell to see that she was gone and so was all of her shit. Where she'd gone, I didn't know and I didn't give a fuck, either.

I went into my bedroom and got dressed so that I could run back out the house. I had to meet with my contractor at my club, Power to make sure that the renovations were going well since we would have to close the club for an extended amount of time.

"We can move the stage from here to the side over here since it creates a better flow with the bar most people frequent," my brother Rashad told the contractor.

My mind wasn't in the meeting since I was tagged in a post on Twitter of Alyssa giving head to some random nigga. I had my eyes glued to the screen watching the video for the fourth time because I was sure she was doing it in my house, in my bed.

"Yo, bro did you hear me?" Rashad asked me.

When I looked up, Rashad and my contractor Ed and brother, Justin were staring at me, waiting for a response but I didn't hear the question. "My bad. I wasn't paying attention. What happened?"

"I was saying, do you think we would have him build that bar on the roof or just leave that space alone?" Rashad asked again.

"Oh, yeah, do the spot on the roof. That shit'll bring in a lot of money. Look, I gotta bounce, but I'm sure that you can take care of this for me. I trust you," I said as I placed my phone back into my pocket.

"Everything all right?" Rashad asked. "Is there something you need me to handle?"

"Nah, just take care of this for me," I replied.

"Rashad will finish walking you through, Ed and afterward, just send me over the plans so we can get this ball rolling."

"You got it, boss," Ed said before I walked out the door.

I was on a mission to find Alyssa's trifling ass. I called my cousin, Courtney. "Where is Alyssa" I barked as soon as she answered the phone.

"Nigga, don't call my phone, yelling at me 'cause you can't find your bitch," Courtney countered.

"You know where she is or not?" I asked.

"She's at my house," Courtney said and I didn't expect to be so easy to get an answer out of her.

"You at home?" I asked as I drive my car in the direction of her house.

"Yeah. You coming here, now?" she queried.

"Yeah, but don't tell Alyssa 'cause I want to talk to her," I said before I hung up and gunned my car to Courtney's house.

When I got there, I beat on that front door like I was the police. My cousin knew exactly where her loyalty lay because I could hear her tell Alyssa to go and answer the door. Alyssa yanked the door open and the look on her face was priceless. I wasn't the type to routinely put my hands on a woman, but the sight of her made me grip her up by her neck. I carried her that way back into the house and slammed her against the wall.

"Bitch, who the fuck you had in my house?" I asked. She didn't answer me, she just stared up at me so I shook her and asked her again. "Who the fuck was that nigga?" Still no response.

I was getting ready to shake her and yell a second time until Courtney yelled, "Let go of her throat so she can speak, damn."

I let Alyssa go when what Courtney said registered and Alyssa dropped down to her knees, gasping for air. I gave her ten seconds before I asked again, "Who the fuck was in my house?"

"I'm not telling you, Melo. Fuck you!" Alyssa said when she got her voice.

"Okay don't tell me, but when I find out, that nigga is dead. And the money I was gonna give you, you can dead that," I told her.

On that note, she popped her ass up with the quickness. "What the fuck do you mean you're not giving me the money?"

I ignored her because I recognized her keys sitting on the table. "I let you take all the clothes and bags and all that other shit I got your ass, but I'm not helping you move on. You better ask that other nigga." I took the key to my house and the key to my BMW that was parked outside.

"I know you're not about to take my car," Alyssa said in shock when she realized what was happening.

I laughed before saying, "You not gonna be riding around with that nigga in my car. All of this could've been simple but you played yourself, Alyssa."

With that, I was out the door. Alyssa was crying as if she wasn't the one at fault. My cousin sat on the couch the entire time watching it all unfold. I knew that she wouldn't interfere, besides, it probably was all entertainment to her.

Afterwards, I needed a drink so I went to the strip club that I was a silent partner in. I had my truck valet parked before I went inside and sat at the bar. Once my presence was noticed by my favorite bartender, Diamond, she came right over. "Who pissed you off today?"

"Why you say that?" I asked with a brow raised.

"Cause that's really the only time you show your face here," Diamond said and I didn't realize that I'd become so predictable.

"Damn, that's crazy. Let me get a double shot of

Henny on the rocks," I said. I didn't feel like sharing about the crazy day that I'd had. I would have never thought it would go so far downhill after it started out so well with me getting Jenae's phone number.

At the thought of Jenae, I pulled out my phone and decided to shoot her text: *What's up?*

Jenae: *Who's this?*

I caught myself getting upset that she didn't know who was texting her until I remember that I never actually gave her my phone number. So, I texted back: *Your future.*

Jenae: *Is this Melo?*

Me: *Yeah. What you doing?"*

Jenae: *I'm just getting in the house from work. What are you up to?*

Me: *I'm at a bar. I want to see you.*

Jenae: *When?*

Me: *Now.*

She didn't respond right away like she had been at the beginning of our conversation. After five minutes, I laid my phone down on the bar but when it vibrated with a text from her: *Okay.*

A smile crept onto my face before I gulped down the rest of my drink and dropped a twenty-dollar bill on the bar. I was getting her address as I walked out the door.

When I pulled up to Jenae's house, she was sitting on the porch alone, looking up at the sky. I wasn't sure if she noticed me walk up until I heard her say, "You ever just look up at the stars and realize how small we are in the universe?"

That question caught me off guard because it seemed like it was from left field. "Nah, I never really did."

She stared up at the sky for a moment longer, before looking at me with a smile on her face. "I didn't really think I'd find myself inviting you to my house."

"Why not?" I asked while looking down at her.

Jenae shrugged. "I've been with the same guy for most of my adult life.

"You still with him?" I asked.

She shook her head from side to side. "No. We broke up."

"What happened?" I quizzed.

"Nothing really happened. He accused me of flirting with you at Justin's party, but then he tried to apologize. I just realized that we were heading in two different directions in life," she explained. There was a sadness in her eyes while she spoke so I wasn't sure how she really felt about it.

"You good?" I asked as I took a seat next to her.

"Yeah," she said as she forced a smile. "It was for the best. It really hasn't hit me yet though, but doubt I that I'll be in bed crying over him."

"Y'all weren't in a good place?" I asked.

Jenae let out a deep sigh before she answered my question. "We were okay, but none of my family really like him and they had good reasons. More than anything, I was just afraid to end things."

"What made you change your mind?"

"Honestly?" she asked as she looked deep into my eyes. "You."

As we stared into each other's eyes, I found myself unable to look away. I grabbed her chin with my hand, gently, and kissed her on the lips. She didn't pull away, at first, but once she realized what was happening, Jenae pulled her head back and covered her mouth with both hands.

"What's wrong?" I asked, hoping that I hadn't overstepped my boundaries.

"I'm sorry, I don't usually do anything like this. I—"

I cut off what she was saying by kissing her again. I didn't want her to think that I was judging her by a single kiss. Also, I couldn't ignore the crazy chemistry that we had. When I pulled away, I said, "You don't have to apologize."

Jenae smiled at me before saying, "You go around just kissing all the girls you meet?"

"Nah, just you. So, you gonna let me come inside, or we chilling out here all night?" I queried. I was tired of sitting on the steps like we were teenagers.

"Ummm…" She turned her head and looked at her house. "I live with my mom and little sister, so I prefer not to."

"Then, come with me to my house," I suggested.

CHAPTER FOUR

JENAE

I couldn't believe that I'd agreed to go with Romelo back to his house. However, it was because of the chemistry we had that I couldn't deny. I kept telling myself over and over again that I wasn't going to have sex with him, but I wasn't sure if I would be able to keep that promise.

"Why you so quiet?" he asked me as we rode in his white Audi R8.

"I don't know," I said as I twirled my long hair around my fingers.

"You nervous? I promise I don't bite," Romelo said to me. "Well, that is unless you want me to."

I looked over at him. "There will be none of that,

sir."

"You want to stop for something to eat or do you want me to pick up a bottle before we get there?"

"Nah. I don't really drink that much and I just ate dinner," I said before I pulled out my phone and started texting Sabrina: *Bitch, why am I in the car with Romelo headed to his house?*

Sabrina: *No, you're not. You gotta be lying.*

Me: *No, I invited him over to my house, but I didn't want to let him inside, so now we're headed to his house since he lives alone. I'm so scared right now.*

Sabrina: *You can't be scared. You got in the car with the nigga.*

Me: *I know. I find myself really liking him, but I don't even know him and we both just got out of relationships.*

Sabrina: *Just go with the flow and if things get crazy, call an Uber. Have fun, chica.*

Me: *Thanks. I'll try and I'll call you tomorrow.*

"You texting your homegirls?" Romelo asked.

Caught, I put my phone into my tote bag. "Yeah, I had to tell Sabrina where I was going, just in case you turn out to be a murderer.

Romelo let out a small chortle. "You think I'm a murderer?"

"No, I don't think you are one, otherwise, I wouldn't be in the car with you right now. However, if my judgment fails me, I need her to know where to tell the police to begin looking for me."

"You wild," Romelo said, still laughing.

"So, tell me about yourself, sir," I said switching the subject.

"What do you want to know?"

"Whatever you want to tell me," I replied. I wanted to know everything about the man I was sitting next to.

"Well, I'm twenty-seven. I enjoy long walks on the beach…"

I hit him playfully on the arm. "Stop playing. I'm serious," I said but I was still giggling.

"What? I really do enjoy long walks on the beach. You don't?" Romelo asked and he had me cracking up.

"I do. I just really want to get to know you and you're acting like you're on a dating site," I responded.

"Okay, then tell me about you if I'm doing all this wrong." He glanced in my direction and suddenly, I know what to say. I thought long and hard, but without a specific question to answer, I was drawing a blank. He picked up on that and said, "See, it's not that easy, is it?"

"Touché. I'm struggling to come up with something witty to say," I admitted.

"How about we start with the basics. How old are you?"

"I'm twenty-two so you have me by like four and a half years because my birthday is in two weeks," I said.

"Really? What's the day?" he asked.

"It's April 29th." I had a smile on my face because the idea of celebrating my birthday was always a big deal for me.

"Wow, that's crazy. My birthday is April 30th."

I gave him the side eye. "You lying."

"Nah, I'm dead serious. So truthfully, I got you by five years, minus a day." The smile on Romelo's face was addictive. It may sound strange to someone who never was blessed to be in his presence, but each time I saw it fade away, I just wanted to do something else to make him smile again.

We pulled up to a two-story house on the opposite side of town than where I stayed. He parked and we got out the car. Romelo surprised me by taking my hand as we walked up to the house. He didn't let go of my hand either when he unlocked the door.

Romelo's house was nice. It was evident that a woman had lived there or at least had a hand in decorating the place. I stepped inside and he directed me to the couch, but my feet wouldn't move.

"What's wrong?" he asked, letting my hand go as he took a seat.

"Your girl...she moved out?" I quizzed as I looked around, kind of expecting her to pop out of a closet or something crazy like that.

"Yeah. I got the key back and everything. You're good here," he said trying to reassure me, but there was a part of me that felt like it was too soon to be in his home. The breakup was still too fresh in my opinion.

"Do you want to go to a hotel? If you're uncomfortable with staying here, I don't want to make you stay."

"Ummm…" I didn't want to seem like I was being difficult, but I didn't want to be there either.

"Come on." Romelo got up and took me by the hand, leading me back out the house.

"Where are we going?" I queried.

"A hotel. You're not comfortable here and that's not what I want."

I didn't say anything else. I just followed Romelo back out the house and to his car. We drove to The Hotel Indigo, downtown. I stood off to the side while he checked us in. We stopped along the way and picked up a bottle of Jack Daniel's Honey Whiskey, so that we'd have something to sip on while we were in the room.

I took a seat at the edge of the bed and held onto my phone moving it from hand to hand as I watched Romelo line the ice bucket with the plastic bag they provided. "I'm going to go get some ice. You good?"

I nodded instead of speaking.

"I'll be right back," Romelo said before he walked out the room.

While he was gone, my phone buzzed in my hand. I looked at it and saw Mike's name along with a picture of us kissing when we were together. I answered it since I was alone. "Hello?"

"Where are you? I'm at your house and your mom said you're not here."

"Why are you at my house? You know we broke up, or did you forget?" I asked confused.

"Yeah, but I thought you were over that shit by now. Can we talk? Your car is here. Did you walk around to Sabrina's house?" Mike probed.

"No. I'm not in the neighborhood," I said as Romelo walked in the room.

"There wasn't that much ice in the machine, but I got as much as I could," Romelo said as he sat the bucket on the dresser.

I smiled at him before I answered Mike. "I don't want to talk, Mike. And, please don't go back around to my house looking for me," I said before hanging up. I had no intentions on talking to him anytime soon. When I sat my phone on the bed and looked up, Romelo was fixing our drinks.

"You smoke?" he quizzed.

"Not really. Sometimes, I do when I'm out with Sabrina, but it's not a regular thing," I replied.

"I'm not Sabrina, but do you want to smoke with me?" he asked as he handed me a glass of the Honey Jack.

I took a sip of the liquor before I responded. "Okay, I guess that's fine."

"Alright. I'm gonna roll this up and then we can go into the bathroom to smoke it."

I nodded as I sipped on my drink. Romelo was an expert at rolling up an el. He had two blunts rolled in mere minutes. He took a towel from the bathroom, put it under the door of the room before we went into the bathroom. Before we could light up, he took another towel, wet it, wrung it out, and put that one under the bathroom door. I watched all his movement intently because I could see his muscles flexing under his blue Champion crew neck t-shirt that he had on.

I sat up on the counter and Romelo turned on the shower before he sat on the closed toilet seat. "Is all of this necessary?" I asked referring to all the towels.

"It's how you avoid that charge for smoking in the room." He lit the blunt, then took a pull. "You good?"

"Yeah. Why you ask me that?"

"Cause you look nervous," he replied with a smile on his face.

I shrugged. "I'm a little nervous. I'll admit that."

"Why?"

"I've had one boyfriend all my life. I've only been alone in this kind of setting with him This is all new to me," I admitted.

"So, you're a goodie goodie?" he asked as he passed me the weed.

I took it and inhaled. I held it for a bit before I exhaled. "I'm not a goodie goodie. I just met Mike when I was really young."

"Basically, that nigga put you on lock before another nigga got the chance to?"

"I guess." I took another pull of the weed before I tried to hand it to Romelo but he wouldn't take it.

"Nah, you can smoke a bit more."

I took another pull and held it while I counted to ten before I passed it back to him. Romelo was still trying to make me keep it but I said, "Nigga if you don't take this."

He laughed at me before taking the blunt out of my hand. He took a pull before asking. "You in school?"

"Nah. I went away to school, but after being there I realized it wasn't for me, so instead of going into debt trying to find myself, I'm working for my cousin at her hair salon."

"So, you do hair?" he asked.

"No. I'm her assistant," I explained.

"What do you want to do with your life, then?" he asked.

"I honestly don't know. I used to want to sing or write songs but I know that realistically that won't happen. Therefore, I'm working for Tracee, my cousin. Maybe one day I'll go to hair school so that I can do hair and make a little more money."

"You can sing?" he asked, skepticism written all over his face.

I nodded. "I'm no Whitney Houston, but I can hold a tune."

"Can you sing for me?" Romelo asked putting me on the spot.

"Right now?" I got nervous about singing for him.

"Yeah, why not?"

I took a deep breath as I tried to think of a song to sing. "Head down, as I watch my feet take turns hitting the ground. Eyes shut, I find myself in love racing the earth. And, I'm soaked in your love. And, love was right in my path, in my grasp. And, me and you belong. I wanna run; smash into you. I wanna run and smash into you." I didn't realize that I had my eyes closed but when I opened them, Romelo was looking at me in awe.

"Damn, what song was that?" he quizzed.

"Smash Into You by Beyonce," I replied.

"You can really sing. I thought you was just gassing and you were gonna sound like Ashanti or some shit but you can really sing. You should go for it," he said. I raised an eyebrow at him causing him to say. "I promise, Jenae, I'm really not gassing you."

"Thank you. I used to put covers of songs up on YouTube but my camera broke and my computer is old as hell, so they would take forever and a day to upload, so I stopped."

"Damn. Niggas be breaking out off of that YouTube shit," Romelo said and I was surprised that he was so interested.

Mike never was interested in anything that interested me. I think he just liked the idea of having a pretty girlfriend by his side. "They really do," I replied.

Romelo handed me the weed before he lit the second one he'd rolled. It was clear that the rest of the blunt was mine, so I took my time smoking it while sipping on my Jack Daniels. "What do you do?"

I quizzed.

"I'm an arms dealer," Romelo said as if it were no big deal.

We weren't in the Middle East so whatever arms he was dealing were of the illegal nature, i.e. illegal guns. I wasn't at all caught off guard nor was I turned off. He was getting money the best way he could. I just hoped that he had bigger plans for the long run. "I also own a couple of clubs. The club that my little brother had his party at was mine, so when you put out your album, you gotta perform there."

I let out a belly laugh. "Oh, okay, sir." By then I was officially on. The weed and liquor had taken their effect and I couldn't stop giggling.

"You okay, Nae?" Romelo asked as he got up from the toilet seat.

I opened my legs so that he could stand between them. I looked up at him while he peered down at me and licked his juicy lips. I couldn't resist the urge to kiss them, so that's exactly what I did. I put my hand on his neck so that I could pull him closer. I was initially the aggressor but that quickly changed as Romelo took control. I allowed his hands to go up under my shirt. I had on a thin knit spaghetti strap top and a lace bralette. Although his hands were on the outside of the bra, since the lace was so thin, it felt like direct contact when he touched my nipples.

I let out a soft moan into his mouth which was a clear indication for Romelo to continue. I had my hand on the waistband of his shorts, debating on if I wanted to go that far with him on the first night. The naughty side of me won. As soon as I reached into his boxers I was shocked by his already hard dick. I didn't have much to compare it to but Romelo was certainly blessed in that department. It was huge and with each stroke, it seemed it get bigger.

I wanted to keep stroking it, but Romelo was picking me up off the counter and carrying me into the bedroom. He laid me down on the bed and pulled off the jeans I was wearing along with my panties. I was panting heavily as he rubbed my clit, which felt like it was swollen.

"You sure you want this?" he asked as he slipped two fingers into my pussy.

"Ohhh yes. I want this," I replied.

"Ain't no turning back," he said before he bent at the waist and sucked my clit into his mouth.

"Fuck!" I moaned as I grabbed hold of the covers. He was a master at eating my pussy, rotating from licking my clit to sucking on it while fingering me at the same time.

I could feel the heat building in my core. I didn't know what was happening to me. The pleasure was too intense that I tried to back away but Romelo wrapped his arms around my legs to keep me in place while he sucked on my clit.

"Oh my God!" I screamed as I had the first orgasm of my life that was achieved by a man and not on my own. Romelo didn't stop eating me out though. I could feel my legs shaking and I needed to get my baring's. I pushed on his head and tried to scoot up the bed until he finally got the point that I couldn't take any more.

Romelo finally took his mouth off my clit and as soon as the air hit it, it started to throb. He climbed up on top of me and placed his mouth on mine. Our tongues danced while we kissed. I was so enthralled in our kiss that I didn't realize he was guiding his dick into my opening. When it slid into me I let out a gasp.

Romelo was huge. I could feel myself being stretched to accommodate him. He must've known that I was trying to adjust to him because he whispered in my ear, "You okay? You want me to stop?"

"No," I replied. With that, he placed another kiss on my lips and gave me slow deliberate strokes until I adjusted and wrapped my legs around him. Once I did that, Romelo lifted up my ass cheeks with his hands and went faster. It felt so good that I didn't even have a voice to be able to moan. My mouth was agape as another orgasm neared.

"Oh my goodness. I'm coming again," I said as I felt so good that I couldn't control myself as I creamed all over his rod.

"That's right," Romelo said sounding out of breath. "Cum on this dick, ma."

I ground my hips into him as he stopped moving. I placed my hands around his neck and then my lips onto his so we could share an intimate kiss.

When Romelo pulled away he said, "You 'bout to make me cum. It's so wet."

I didn't care if he came or not. It was feeling too good for me to stop rotating my hips. Slowly, Romelo pulled out of me and bent down to eat my pussy again. This time I held onto the top of his head and ground my pelvis onto his face so that I could reach my third orgasm of the night. When I came, he didn't stop licking my clit until I was coming again. That's when he said, "Turn over."

I turned over and stuck my ass in the air. I expected to feel him guiding his penis back inside but instead, I felt his tongue probing my vagina. It took everything in me to keep from screaming out in pleasure. When I came, I could feel it squirting out on the bed. That was when he entered me. Romelo was so deep that I had to bite the pillow. It was the perfect mix of pleasure and pain as he pounded into me, smacking my ass.

I came once again and my legs went out from under me but he didn't miss a beat. He just laid his body on mine and kept stroking me. "Ooh, Romelo, it feels so good."

"You like this dick?"

"Yeah. It's so big," I managed to reply.

"This my pussy now, Nae?" he asked.

"Yeah, it's yours. Fuck your pussy, baby," I said as I started to throw it back. Upon hearing that Romelo went faster until I heard him grunt before he came inside of me. Thankfully, I was on birth control. Once Romelo was off of me, I got up and went to the bathroom. I knew that I was hot and sweaty. The worst part was that I still had on my shirt and bra. I peeled them both off and laid them on the sink before I hopped in the shower. I'd gotten the temperature just right when Romelo joined me, placing kisses on the back of my neck. "Noooo, she needs time to recoup," I said referring to my peach which had to be bruised from the beating he's put on me.

"Don't worry. I'm not going to do anything you

don't want me to."

I turned around so that I could look him in the eye. "Okay," I said before our lips met for a kiss.

ROMELO

Jenae looked up at me with her big doe eyes and believe it or not, I knew at that moment she would be my wife. I knew she was the one for me. I never believed in any shit like that until that moment. I could tell that she felt the same way. We just stood there for a moment, taking each other in before I kissed her on the lips.

After showering, Jenae wrapped herself in the terry cloth robe that was hanging up in the closet before she sat down Indian style on the bed. I put my boxers back on and sat down before I turned on the TV. I didn't plan on watching it. I just wanted background noise. I was just about to say something when my cell phone rang. I picked it up and noticed it was Antoine calling me.

"Nigga, where are you?" he quizzed.

"I'm chilling at the moment. You need something?"

"Alyssa dumb ass up here at the club acting like a fool right now. You might want to come and get her to take her home. Black took her to the office to get to calm down but she tripping for real, bro," Antoine explained.

"I ain't fucking with her no more so y'all can kick her out if y'all need to," I said. I didn't want to go down to the club if I didn't need to.

"Man…" Antoine started to say, making it clear that he didn't want to deal with Alyssa either.

"Fuck, I'm on my way," I said before I hung up.

"Everything okay?" Jenae asked me with a look of concern on her face.

"Nah. Alyssa's at one of my clubs and I gotta go take care of it. You staying here or coming with me?" I asked as I put my clothes back on.

"I'm coming. I don't want to stay here all by myself," she responded as she stood up and took off her robe. Jenae was naked under it and I couldn't help but admire her body because it was seriously a work of art. Her skin was all the same chocolate tone, no imperfections or blemishes. Jenae's titties weren't small but they weren't too big either and they were perky as hell. If I didn't have to rush to my club I'd be popping one of her nipples in my mouth.

I sighed and continued to get dressed since I couldn't do anything with her. Jenae had to get her shirt and bra from the bathroom. When she came back out she was fully dressed and trying to smooth her hair out with her hands but that shit was all over her head and frizzy from our activities. I was putting on my sneakers while she was raking her hair up into a ponytail at the top of her head. With her hair up and out of her face, she was even more beautiful. I didn't even know that was possible.

"I'm ready," Jenae said once she was dressed, with her phone in her hand.

"Okay, let's go."

I parked the car in the back of the club and walked inside. It was a Thursday night but it was jumping as if it were a Friday or Saturday. We hadn't yet closed for renovations since the plans were still being drawn up. I held Jenae's hand tight as I went to find Antoine. He was standing outside of my office and I could hear Alyssa inside yelling. You would've thought that after all that time had passed, she would've calmed down by then, but she had stamina.

"Man, what the fuck is going on?" I asked Antoine.

Antoine didn't answer me right away because he was looking Jenae up and down.

"Nigga, what's happening with Alyssa?"

"She got her early and got drunk then started fighting with one of the bartenders. Black carried her in here and she said that she wasn't going anywhere until you got here."

"Rashad not here?" I quizzed because my little brother knew how to take care of these type of things.

"Naw, he ain't come in tonight," Antoine replied.

"Fuck man," I said before I opened my office door. Black was sitting behind my desk in the chair while Alyssa was yelling at him.

"Tell that motherfucker to get down here!" she screamed at the top of her lungs.

"I'm here. Now what you want?" I asked stepping into the office still holding Jenae's hand although she was trying to step out the office and avoid confrontation with Alyssa.

Alyssa's breath caught in her throat once she noticed Jenae. "So, you got a new bitch that quick?"

"Who she calling a bitch?" Jenae asked me. From the way she was originally trying to keep from walking in the office, I thought she may have been scary, but that clearly wasn't the case.

"I'm talking about you, bitch," Alyssa replied.

"I don't know you and I'm not trying to go there with you, however, you're not gonna keep calling me a bitch," Jenae said. She remained calm as she spoke and my mom always told me to watch out for chicks that stayed calm in tense situations because they usually would finish whatever fight was started.

"And if I don't, bitch?" Alyssa antagonized.

"Melo, you really need to get her because I don't want to be disrespectful to you right now," Jenae replied, looking up at me.

"He can't do shit right now. Besides I'm talking to you right now, bit—"

Alyssa didn't get to finish that word because Jenae punched her dead in the mouth, drawing blood right away. Alyssa was surprised because she was used to running her mouth and other bitches being too shook to lay hands on her. It was clear that Jenae wasn't the typical female that would fight with wild swings and hair pulling. That girl had hands. That was clear to Alyssa as well because she didn't even try to retaliate, she just walked out the office holding her leaking mouth.

Still, Jenae was calm, cool, and collected. She grabbed my hand again once Alyssa was out the room. "Can we go now?" she asked.

"Yeah." That shit turned me the fuck on. I'd never seen anything like it before and Black and Antoine were standing there looking on in awe.

Once we were back in my car, Jenae rubbed her hand. "Her teeth hit my knuckle."

"You good?" I quizzed.

"Oh yeah. I'm fine. I'm sorry about that but I couldn't let her disrespect me like that," Jenae said looking at me with those eyes again. She looked so innocent but I could tell there was a beast buried deep down.

"How you learn to throw a punch like that?"

"I took up boxing for a bit when I was in high school but once they tried to get me to actually fight in the ring, I stopped. I just wanted to learn to defend myself. Bitches used to fuck with me for no reason, so if I had to fight, I was going to do some real damage," she explained.

I smiled because I knew that I would enjoy getting to know her. She was nothing like any other girl I'd ever dealt with.

JENAE

I hated fighting but I hated being disrespected even more, which is why I punched Alyssa. It was out of pure reflex. Now, my knuckle was throbbing because her teeth were hard as hell. That was what I got for trying to knock them out her mouth, though. "Are we going back to the room or are you taking me home?"

"Do you have to work in the morning?" he queried.

"Yeah. I'm supposed to work," I replied.

"We can go back to the room. If you want I can stop by your house so you can get a change of clothes for tomorrow."

"That would be nice. Thank you." I sat back in the leather seats while I watched the city go by as we headed to my house.

Once there, it was 1:15 in the morning. I used my key to let myself inside and was quiet as possible as I headed up to my room. I was pulling out a pair of jeans from my bottom drawer when my little sister came in.

"Where are you going?" she quizzed.

"Out," I replied.

"With the nigga parked in that Benz out there?" she probed.

"Yeah. I'll see you tomorrow," I said throwing my outfit for tomorrow into my Louis Vuitton Neverfull. I walked over to my dresser to get toiletries and my brush, but Leilani was still staring at me. "What?"

"You spending the night with him?"

"Yeah, which is why I'm packing a bag."

"What's his name?"

"Damn, I can't have any secrets around here, huh? I'm not about to play twenty-one questions with you Lani," I said as I threw my bag over my shoulder.

"Okay, but when you come back home, I better get the tea," Leilani demanded.

"That's if I come back," I joked sticking my tongue out. I ran out the house and got into Romelo's car. I placed my bag in the back seat after I closed the door, then put on my seatbelt. As soon as my left hand was free, he held it before pulling off from the parking spot.

We went to his house, where I waited in the car while he grabbed a change of clothes. Back at the hotel, we barely got the door closed before we were all over each other and round two was started.

"You on birth control?" Romelo asked as we were lying in bed after our second shower of the evening.

"Yeah," I replied. I was looking up at the ceiling thinking about everything that happened.

"Good. I probably should have asked that sooner," he replied.

I turned on my side so that I could get a good look at him. "Do you think that we're moving too fast? Or is this just a fuck buddy situation?"

"What do you want it to be?" he asked placing the ball back in my court.

"I've never had a fuck buddy before. I'm not sure if I know what the rules are," I joked. "But, nah, I like you, which surprises me because I was with my ex for so long."

"How you stay with that nigga so long if he didn't even know how to make you cum?" Romelo asked.

"'Cause sex is about more than orgasms," I replied.

"That's bullshit. Yeah, it's a connection with another person, but the end goal is to cum. I don't even consider it sex if I don't nut."

I laughed. "I like to think that it's about the connection."

"That's 'cause you weren't doing it right. But stick with the kid and I'll teach you a few things."

THREE WEEKS LATER

"I thought you were joking about never coming back home. I haven't seen you in a month of Sundays and you're here to get clothes. Who is this guy that's stolen my sister?" Leilani said as she sat on the edge of my bed, watching me put clothes into my Louis Vuitton duffle bag.

"His name is Romelo and I really like spending time with him."

"The only Romelo I know is the one that owns the clubs."

"Yup, that's him," I replied.

"Bitch, you lying. I been checking your Instagram faithfully trying to see if you posted him, but nothing. How did y'all meet?"

"I met him at the mall, believe it or not."

"Well, you better put that nigga on your IG so that these thirsty hoes know he's taken. I want to see y'all interact. It's weird to think of you with someone other than Mike," Leilani said.

"Okay. You can come with me to Melo's club tomorrow night. It's the last night before it closes for renovations, so it's going to be lit as hell. Plus, it's my birthday so you know that I want you there for sure. But, I gotta go because he's waiting for me at home. We're supposed to go out to dinner." I zipped up my bag, kissed my little sister on the cheek and bounced.

I still needed to get to Romelo's place so that I could shower and get dressed. After the first couple of nights at the hotel, Romelo convinced me that Alyssa wasn't going to show up at his house unannounced as so far, he was right. It was probably because she didn't want to catch these hands a second time. It did bother me that I was sleeping in a bed that he shared with another woman, but I didn't live there so I hadn't said anything about it.

When I got to the house, I knocked on the door and was surprised to see Romelo's cousin Antoine answering it. "Hey, Antoine," I said as I stepped inside. "Is Melo here?"

"Yeah, he upstairs. That nigga ain't give you a key yet? You basically live here," he said as he went to sit back on the couch and continued playing Grand Theft Auto.

I shrugged. "I don't know. Ask your boy why I

don't have one, yet," I said before I headed upstairs to find Romelo on the phone in his bedroom. "Hey baby," I said before I kissed him on the lips.

I threw my bag on the bed so I could take out the clothes I wanted to wear out to dinner while I eavesdropped on his conversation.

"No, tell that nigga the same thing I just told you. I don't front nobody shit. If he wants it he will have to pay up front. If he doesn't, then he can for sure go elsewhere, but ain't nobody else going to front him shit either... Nah, don't tell him to call me unless he's ready to pay up front... Alright, I gotta go." Romelo got off the phone and said to me, "You getting dressed over here?"

"Yeah. I told you that I was just going home to get some more clothes," I replied. "We're still on for dinner, right?"

"Of course. I gotta step out for a second, but we can to as soon as I come back."

"Umm... okay," I said confused because I thought we would be going as soon as I was dressed. "How long you gonna be?"

"I gotta go to Dorchester real quick, then I'll be back. I promised I'll make it quick."

"Okay, well, I'll be there," I replied. I slipped my

jeans off and sat on the bed. My phone was ringing and Mike's name was flashing on the screen. However, by then I'd deleted the picture of us kissing, but with the amount of times Mike continued to call each day, I was on the verge of putting his ass on the block list.

"That nigga still calling you?" Romelo asked, looking down at my phone.

"Yeah. I'm about to block him because it's getting annoying," I replied as I touched the decline button on the screen.

"Have you spoken to him since y'all broke up?" he queried.

"No, especially since he left me that voicemail, calling me all types of names because he heard your voice. His reaction is why I keep shit so personal," I replied. I hated being judged just for living my life.

"Is that why you ain't post me on your Instagram or won't even follow me back, for that matter?" Romelo asked.

"I didn't even know that you cared about that stuff. I'll follow you back. You know I like to stay low key. You're the flashy one, always posting your outfits and shit, but you never posted me either," I retorted.

"How would you know? You don't follow me."

I giggled before I answered him. "I may not follow you but I still check your page on the daily."

"Okay, well while you're sitting there, follow your nigga back," Romelo said pointing down at my phone.

I picked up my phone and went straight to his page, once I was on Instagram. "There, I've followed you back. But since when did you become my nigga. I don't remember us making anything official," I said and I was dead serious but Romelo was laughing.

"The moment I slip up in there, we made shit official. You're mine," he said.

"I'm yours, but are you mine? This isn't a one-sided thing, is it?" I quizzed.

"No, I'm yours too," he said as he inched closer to me.

Romelo climbed on top of me and started kissing me. I opened my legs so I could wrap them around him. As he reached down to touch my panty covered clit, we heard, "Yo, bro, you ready to go?"

"Fuck," Romelo said with his lips still on mine, before he pecked them and stood up. "I forgot that nigga was down there. I'll be back in like an hour."

"Okay. Be safe, babe," I said as I watched him leave.

CHAPTER FIVE

SABRINA

"I haven't seen your ass in two weeks. Is Romelo holding you hostage? I even went to the shop to get my hair done by Tracee but you weren't there," I said to my best friend. "Nikki had to shampoo my hair."

"Sorry girl, but he's not holding me hostage. I've been to work but I called out last Saturday night because I was out late with Melo in some club in Philly. You still coming to his club tomorrow though, right?" she asked.

"Yeah. You already got something to wear?" I quizzed. I wanted to see her and catch up before we went to the club and the music was too loud for us to actually talk and for me to get all the tea on her new situation.

"No, I stopped by my house to look for something but this party is being talked about all over Baltimore. I need to look as fly as possible," she replied.

"Good. Pick me up from work tomorrow so we can go shopping," I said.

"Tuh," Jenae said before laughing. "How you just gonna tell me what to do?"

"Can you pick me up from work so we can find outfits together?" I said rephrasing it into a question.

"That's better. Sure, Bree, I have no problem picking you up from work. I should get out of the shop early myself. What time do you get off?" Jenae asked.

"At 4:30. What you doing, right now?"

"Laying in the bed at Melo's house. I should be getting dressed for dinner, but he ran out so I'm being lazy, right now."

"When the last time you been home?" I asked because every time I talked to her she was at that nigga's house. Mike had stopped by my apartment like six times in the past three weeks, looking for her.

"I was there today to get clothes, but that's really it. I've been here every night since the first night we spent together."

"So, you living there, now?"

"No. I just really enjoy sleeping in his arms," Jenae said and I could tell she was blushing.

"Bitch, you live there now, no matter what you say," I declared. I heard a knock on the door and got u to answer it. When I looked out the peephole, I saw Mike standing there. I sighed and then said into the phone, "Bitch, your ex keeps showing up at my damn door. Can you tell him about you and Romelo being together so that he'll leave me the fuck alone?"

"What? Tell that nigga to go the fuck away. I don't have to tell him because he already knows. That nigga is just plain crazy. Matter of fact, don't even answer the door for his dumb ass."

I couldn't just not answer the door mainly because I was sure he heard me speaking to her on the phone. "I'm opening the door." I unlocked my door and swung it open to see Mike standing on the other side. He looked rough and I almost pitied him but then I remembered that he was the definition of a fuckboy. "She not here, Mike."

"Man, do you know where the hell she is? I just want to talk to her and apologize," Mike said in a somber tone.

"She's been staying with her boyfriend, Romelo. I don't think she wants to talk."

When I said that I could hear Jenae yell, "Don't tell him that."

"Can you tell her that I was looking for her, the next time you see her," Mike pleaded.

"Yeah, but in the meantime, stop coming by here 'cause Nae ain't even been here in a month," I explained.

"Aight," Mike said before walking off.

I closed the door, then said, "Bitch, you should've seen his face. He looked so damn pitiful."

"I don't care. When will he get the hint that I'm all the way through?" she quizzed.

"Probably, when you tell him yourself."

"Welp, that's never going to happen," she answered. "Oh shit! Romelo just came home and I haven't even jumped in the shower yet. I gotta go. I'll call you, tomorrow."

"Okay. Have fun at dinner," I said before getting off the phone.

I was officially bored once I got off the phone

with Jenae. Justin was at a baseball game with his friend and wouldn't be coming over. I tried to watch Netflix, but that was boring as well, so I called Erykah, my older sister and invited her over.

"Knock, knock," I heard Erykah say as she rang my doorbell.

I basically ran to the door to open it. I was going to pull her in for a hug, but her arms were full since she was carrying a box of pizza and had a bag with wine draped on her arm. "Hi, sissy," I said as I took the pizza from her. I went and sat it on my small dining room table. I lifted the top up off the box and was hit with a bunch of steam before I saw that it was a pepperoni pizza. Instantly, my stomach growled and I grabbed a slice without bothering to get either of us a plate.

"Hungry much?" Erykah quizzed.

"You know damn well, I can't resist pizza," I said before I took a bite. It burnt the hell out of the roof of my mouth, but I didn't care. "I missed you though, Erykah. I'm so glad you could come over."

"I'm glad you invited me," she said taking a seat at the table with me. "How are things with the new boo?"

"They're going good. He's on the straight and narrow and I'm not used to it."

"But isn't he one of the Moore brothers? I mean, isn't his brother Melo heavy in the streets? How much of a square can he really be?" Erykah asked me.

"Yeah, he's Romelo's little brother, but Romelo sent him off to school. He was the only one who actually stayed," I told her.

"Oh, I see. You been around Melo's fine ass, yet? I heard he broke up with his girl. You should hook your sister up. I need a nigga with his kind of money in my life," Erykah said raising her brows for emphasis.

"Sorry, but I can't. He's actually with Jenae."

"Really?" Erykah asked before sucking her teeth. "You hooked them up, didn't you?"

"Nope. That was all the universe at work. He really likes her too. She's basically living at his house."

"Oh, damn, they're moving fast. I would be upset since it's Jenae. I'm happy for her. I bet that nigga is going to spoil the shit out of her too."

"From what Justin told me, that's his goal."

ROMELO

I was walking up the stairs when I heard the shower turn on. I fully expected Jenae to already be dressed once I returned but obviously, that wasn't the case. I went into the bedroom and undressed so I could get in the shower with her. I figured it would be a good idea to conserve water.

I pulled back the shower curtain and she let out a little yelp, in surprise. "You got here fast," Jenae said as she poured soap onto her shower puff or whatever that girly shit was called.

"Actually, I was gone or an hour and a half," I said with a half-smile.

"Oh, I was on the phone with Bree and time got away from me. I didn't say you could get in the shower with me, though," she said.

"But, I'm not getting out," I said as I took the puff out of her hand and started to wash her body for her. Once I'd got the front, she turned around so I could wash her back.

When Jenae rinsed off, she turned back around to face me and looked me in the eyes, before she stood up on her toes to kiss me.

"Don't go starting something you can't finish," I warned her.

"I'm not starting anything," she said with a smile on her pretty face. "It's just a kiss."

"Just a kiss?" I asked as I put my hand between her legs and slipped a finger into her slit while I used my thumb to rub her clit.

Jenae dropped her head back in ecstasy, leaving neck exposed for me to kiss it. She moaned out loud while she rotated her hips on my hand. When she said, "I'm about to cum," I stopped. The look she gave me when I pulled my hand away was priceless. "Why did you stop?"

"'Cause, we gotta get ready for dinner, right? Or did you want to skip dinner and go straight to dessert?"

"What do you think?" she asked as she grabbed my dick and started to stroke it.

'I'm a little hungry," I said trying not to give in.

"So, what," Jenae said as she got on her hands and knees before enveloping me into her warm mouth. It was her first time giving me head and I had to hold onto the wall to keep my damn knees from buckling. "Fuck," I groaned.

She was deep throating me while moaning,

causing a vibration on the tip of my dick. When she pulled it out, she twirled her tongue on the tip before sucking it into her mouth again, this time with a vacuum like suction. Jenae bobbed her head up and down until I was forced to pull away so I wouldn't cum before I got to feel her wet walls.

"Turn around," I demanded and she did so, propping her leg up on the side of the tub, giving me easy access. I lifted her right cheek and slid in. I didn't move for a moment because I wanted to relish in the feeling, but Jenae wasn't going for that because she started to slowly throw it back. Therefore, I gave her long slow strokes while I played with her clit. I kept that same slow, measured pace until Jenae moaned, "I'm coming."

As soon as she got hers, I went full force until I was exploding inside of her. I pulled out and caught my breath before we finished showering.

JENAE

"So, where are we going?" I asked once I was dressed in a navy blue dress that exposed back.

"We can find a restaurant at the harbor. I wanted to spend some alone time with you since your birthday is tomorrow and we'll be at the club," Romelo said.

I smirked because I should've known that was why we were going out in the first place. We'd both decided to have the last night at the club before our joint unofficial birthday party. "Aww, babe. That's what's up."

He laughed at my reaction before he asked, "You ready?"

"Yeah, just let me put my shoes on," I said before I sat on the bed so I could put on my black Balenciaga booties.

Romelo pulled out his white Audi R8. That was the best car in his collection. He opened my door for me and I climbed inside. Romelo held onto my hand as we drove in the direction of the harbor. The restaurant he selected was The Capital Grille. It was my favorite restaurant but he had no way of knowing that, so there was a huge smile on my face.

"Why you looking like that?" he asked as he killed the engine.

"This is my favorite restaurant," I admitted.

Romelo smiled at me and his smile was just as bright as the one I was sporting. "Really, that's crazy. I never been here before, but I heard it was good, so I wanted to come."

"We just be vibing, huh?" I said because our connection was crazy and our chemistry was off the charts.

"We really are though," he said as he got out the car. I waited patiently for him to come and open the door for me before taking my hand and helping me out of the car. It took some getting used to, but Romelo was such a gentleman, especially when we were in public. I never touched a door. He always walked on the outside, when we were on the sidewalk. He held my hand all the time and most importantly, I was never to touch the bill when we went somewhere.

We walked up to the door of the restaurant hand in hand and when we reached the hostess station, Romelo surprised me by saying, "I have an 8:45 reservation under the last name Moore."

"Oh, yes, Mr. Moore, right this way, the hostess said as she grabbed two menus and took us to a table near the back of the restaurant.

"You had reservations?" I asked blushing a little once we were seated.

"Yeah, I made them on my way over here online, that way we ain't have to wait," he explained bursting my bubble.

"Oh, that's what's up," I said trying to play it off. "So, if you and I are officially celebrating my birthday today, did you get me a gift?"

"Nah, you're gonna have to wait until tomorrow for that. Justin said you going shopping with Sabrina tomorrow?" he asked as he looked over the menu.

"Yeah. I'm not working tomorrow, but I have to go get my hair done, but after that, I'm picking her up. Why?" I quizzed. I didn't need to look down at the menu. I knew exactly what I was going to order.

"I was just checking. I gotta get you a key to the house so that you don't have to wait around for me to get in. I'm not sure if I'll be around during the day. I've got a couple of meetings before I can get ready, myself."

"A key?" I asked putting my hand to my chest, clutching my imaginary pearls. "I'm special enough to get a key?"

"You're a damn fool, yo. Yeah, you might as well get your things from your mom's house so you can move in too. I don't want you not sleeping next to me every night," Romelo said and I had a feeling that was coming.

I put my index finger up because I had something important to say. "I'm sorry, but if you want me to move, in, I need you to get a new bed. Sometimes when I lay in it, all I can think about is Alyssa, which is why I think she might've done some Hoodoo on it. I wouldn't be surprised if you lifted it up and see some evidence of it."

"Hoo-what?" Romelo asked me looking at me as if he'd thought I'd lost my damn mind.

"Hoodoo, conjure magic. It's like voodoo, but not really. My granny in Louisiana practices it and I'm telling you, I felt that shit the first time I went to your house, that's why I put salt around the bed and brick dust at the door of the house."

"You're playing with me right now, right?" he asked, eyes wide as hell.

"No, nigga. I called my granny because I really didn't feel right in that house at first. I don't practice it, but that girl spelled you, I promise."

"I wouldn't be surprised if she really did. I wanted to end thing with her for long as fuck but I couldn't do it. That's crazy."

I shrugged. "I don't blame her, though. I'm not about to let anything get between us either."

"You ain't spell me or whatever that shit is, did you?"

"Hell no. I didn't even want your ass at first, remember?"

"Now you all over the kid," he joked.

"I sure am," I said, blushing.

Romelo sat across from me and looked me in the eye. "I love you, Nae."

My heart skipped a beat when he said those three words, but I felt exactly the same way. "I love you too and truth be told, it scares me."

The waiter walked up just as Romelo was about to respond. We place our order and as soon as he walked off, Romelo spoke. "Why are you scared to love me?"

"Because I knew that I loved you since the first night we were together and that's just crazy. And, it wasn't just because he had sex. I love you since that first kiss we shared. I didn't know it was possible but I'm just so drawn to you," I said pouring my heart out to her.

"I've known since then as well. I just didn't want

to scare you off or make you think I wanted to get in your panties but I been knew that I loved your crazy ass."

"Crazy? How am I crazy?" I quizzed.

"How are you not? You fucked Alyssa up that night and now you're talking about Voodoo and Santeria as if it's normal. That's cool, though," Romelo said laughing and I couldn't help but laugh along with him because when he put it that way, I did sound crazy.

The rest of dinner was nice and we took the long way home, with the top down. We drove through the streets of Baltimore while I looked up at the stars through the skylight. For the first time, I was content with the way my life was going.

CHAPTER SIX

ROMELO

I got out of bed, doing my best not to wake Jenae, although it wasn't too hard. She was a super deep sleeper. I didn't want to get out of bed. I didn't want to take my arms from around her, but I did. I had to. There was money to be made. It was 6:15 in the morning but I had to drive out to meet a customer in D.C. and the earlier I got out the house the better.

I threw on an Armani Exchange sweat suit and headed to my warehouse where I kept the inventory I was sitting on. I tried to keep a few weapons on hand so that not too many would be able to be traced back to me. That way, if the 'Alphabet Boys' ever swooped in, it wouldn't be too bad for me. Once in my warehouse, I put the order together and headed to pick up Antoine so that we could ride together. "Yo, what's up with you and Jenae? You really feeling her?"

"Yeah. Why?" Something about Antoine's tone seemed off to me.

"If I told you that, I heard some shit about her..." my cousin trailed off.

"Heard something, like what?" My eyes glanced over at him, then back on the road.

"Nah, I'm just fucking with you. I ain't hear no shit about her, cuz. What's up with Alyssa, though? You heard from her at all?" Antoine was a clown, for real. That nigga played way too much.

"Nah. I ain't hear nothing from Alyssa since Jenae damn near broke her jaw."

"You know she's running around the city with Phil's nut ass," Antoine said and that was news to me.

"That's not a good look for her, but I honestly don't give a fuck. As long as she stays away from me and my girl, she can fuck whoever she likes," I said and I meant every single word. When we were first breaking up, I didn't want to be mean to her but she was on some disrespectful shit so I didn't give a fuck about her."

"I hear you. It just don't look good for you

either," Antoine replied.

"I don't give a fuck about that either," I replied.

We met up with my customer, Nathan, then booked it back up to Baltimore so that I could get ready for the party that was happening later that night. I dropped off Antoine and with it being Jenae's actual birthday, I had to pick up her gifts. I was going all out too. She was riding around in was a '07 Hyundi Sonata and I wanted to give her an upgrade. Jenae had swag already. That was undeniable, but I wanted her swag to match my own. It was only right.

"What you getting?" Justin asked me as we walked into the Mercedes-Benz dealership.

"A new car for, Nae. She's still driving around in a car that her last nigga got her. I already put in the order for a white E550 Cabriolet with a black interior. That shit is pure fire. Its ready for me to pick up today, which is perfect. I just need you to drive it over to your house for me. I don't want her to find out yet," I explained. I knew that Jenae would be excited about the car. I couldn't wait to see the look on her face when I gave it to her.

"An E550 Cabriolet? Yo, you must really like her. You were with Alyssa for years and you never went all out for her like this," Justin said.

He was right. I took care of Alyssa and for average standards, she had it good, but I didn't spoil her, not the way that I planned on spoiling Jenae. Jenae and Alyssa were two different type of women, with Jenae being on a different level entirely. When you find the one, you just know," I replied.

"The one? Nigga, you thinking of marriage already?" Justin asked, stopping right in place.

"Nah, I mean that she's the one I want to spoil, nigga," I said although I was really thinking about marriage, heavily. I just wasn't sure if I was ready to admit it out loud.

"Oh, you had a nigga shook for a second," Justin chided.

"Why the fuck would you be shook? You wouldn't be getting married. Anyway, let's just get this car 'cause I still got a bunch of shit to take care of before I go to Power tonight."

Because I was only picking up the car and all the paperwork was already taken care of, Justin and I were only at the dealership twenty minutes, tops. After warning Justin to make sure he didn't get a single scratch on Jenae's car, we separated. I was supposed to be getting my hair cut, but I had to make one quick stop first.

JENAE

I was a bit disappointed when I woke up because Romelo was already gone. I just knew I'd be blessed with some birthday sex, but unfortunately, that wasn't the case. I laid in the bed for a moment before I finally reached under my pillow and retrieved my iPhone. Naturally, there were a ton of text messages from people wishing me a happy birthday. I opened my mom's first and she sent a sweet message about the day I entered her life, making me one of the biggest blessings she received in her life next to my siblings. The next message I opened was Leilani's and she was just as sentimental as my mother.

Sabrina was turned all the way up as if it weren't eight in the morning when she sent me the text message. In true Sabrina fashion, it was a voice message sent through iMessage. "Happy Birthday, bitch!" she yelled. "I can't wait to see you when I get off work. Love you. We gonna turn the fuck up, tonight."

I didn't even reply with a thank you. Instead, I sent half a dozen of the crying laughing face emojis. I read the message that Romelo sent me, next: *Happy Birthday, beautiful. I had to make a quick run, but I'll be back once I take care of shit. It will be before the party. If you look in the nightstand, there's five stacks in it so you can get an outfit for tonight. I love you.*

Romelo, I texted right back: *Thank you, babe. I love you too.*

I got myself up and out of bed, finally and went to take a shower. I had to get to the salon. I wasn't walking and Tracee promised that she would do my hair for me. I threw on an Adidas Original floral tracksuit before I drove down to Tracee's salon.

Tracee had flowers and balloons waiting for me at the blow dry station. "Happy Birthday, Nae-Nae," she said before embracing me in a hug.

"Thank you," I said. Once she released me from the hug, I noticed that Leilani was at the salon getting braided up by the second assistant, Anastasia. "Lani, what you doing here?"

I went and stood in front of her as I pulled my ponytail down from the top of my head.

"I need my hair done for tonight. My new boo is friends with Romelo so he invited me out tonight too."

Leilani having a new boo was news to me. If he was friends with Romelo then most likely he was older. She had just turned twenty-one so I was still overprotective of my baby sister. "What is his name and why didn't you tell me about him?"

"Keraun and we both have been busy so it never really came up," she replied, blushing.

"How long you been dealing with him?" I quizzed.

Leilani shrugged. "Like six months or so."

"Bitch, that ain't new. You been holding out on me but got the nerve to be all up in my shit," I said.

"That's cause I'm not trying to hear you say that he's too old for me," was Leilani's response.

"How old is he, then?" I quizzed, nervous of what the answer would be.

"Twenty-nine," she replied.

"Oh, I was afraid that you were gonna say like thirty-five but twenty-nine isn't too bad." Tracee was in the back of the salon standing at the shampoo bowl so I sat down but that didn't stop me from running my mouth. "I never heard of Keraun. I only know a few friends though, but I'm excited to meet him. He got any kids?"

"Nae, if you don't sit back so I can shampoo your damn hair," Tracee said before Leilani could speak.

"Oh, my bad," I sat back so that Tracee could get started.

"He got kids but he don't have a crazy baby mom. She actually seems nice," Leilani said finally able to answer my question.

"That's what's up," I said before I shut my mouth to enjoy the special treatment I was getting. Tracee never shampooed hair, which is why she had two assistants yet she was shampooing mine and it was so relaxing.

I was getting my natural hair pressed out with a few clip-ins added for fullness and a couple extra inches in the back. My hair naturally stopped just at the top of my bra strap and with the clip-ins, it was just below my bra strap.

Leilani was getting her hair in a full sew-in with her top out. Her hair was just a little bit shorter than mine, but she was getting bundles down her back. All of her tresses were dyed a honey blonde, color, which complemented her caramel complexion. Our parents had some good genes. While I took after our father in my chocolate color, Leilani was the mirror image of my mother with hazel eyes and full pouty lips. The two of them were breathtakingly gorgeous.

"You coming to the club, tonight?" I asked Tracee.

"For the thousandth time, yes. I'll be there. I even made sure that I take my last person early," Tracee said. It was a regular thing for her to miss an event because she was stuck in the salon or exhausted from a day of work.

"Yay. I'm super excited now," I said.

I was officially in Tracee's chair while Leilani was waiting for me to finish up since she wanted to come along with me to pick up Sabrina from work. That way we all could go shopping together. Tracee was pressing out my hair while I texting Romelo: *Hey babe.*

Romelo: *What's up?*

Me: *Nothing. I'm at the salon getting my hair done.*

Romelo: *You good?*

Me: *Yeah. I'm just hungry. I can't wait until I get out of here so I can get something to eat.*

Romelo: *I'm in the neighborhood. You want me to bring you something?*

Me: *Aww, babe, that would be great. Can you bring me some Popeye's butterfly shrimp and a strawberry Fanta?*

Romelo: *Okay, I'll be there in like twenty minutes.*

Me: *Thank you.*

"Why are you smiling so damn hard?" Leilani asked me as I sat my phone on my lap.

"Melo's bringing me something to eat," I replied.

"I should have known that it had something to do with food," Leilani replied, knowing me all too well.

"You know it," I said.

Romelo: *I'm here. Come outside.*

I read the text from him and replied: *I can't. I'm in the chair.*

Romelo: *Okay, I'm coming in.*

My man looked good as hell when he came in. Romelo had a pair of black jeans and a crisp white v-neck t-shirt, with a red leather motorcycle jacket and his oversized aviator gold glasses with clear lenses. He came over and handed me the food before he gave me a kiss on the lips.

"Thanks, babe," I said.

"You got it," he said. "You gonna have her looking good, right," Romelo asked Tracee.

"Yeah, of course," Tracee replied.

"Good, cause it's a big night for us," Romelo said before he turned to leave. "Oh shit, Lani. I ain't even see you over there."

"You know my little sister?" I asked.

"Yeah," Romelo said turning to me. "Keraun's my homie so of course I know Lani. I ain't even know that she as your little sister."

"That's my baby sister so Keraun better be a good guy."

"He's good people, Nae," Romelo said with a small laugh.

"I told you that I knew him, Jenae," Leilani interjected.

"I thought you meant you knew of him, not that you knew him," I said to her.

"What time you gonna be back home?" Romelo asked.

"Like nine. That's fine?"

"Yeah. I'll see you when you get home." Romelo kissed me on the lips before he left.

I was only in the salon for another forty-five minutes before we were able to go pick up Sabrina from work. We arrived just in time to pick her up.

Sabrina jumped into my backseat and said, "Y'all look so cute and I got this old ass weave in. It's all good though. I'll get you to fix me up, Nae. Oh, we gotta pick up Erykah too, so that she can come with us."

"And where is Erykah?" I quizzed as I started to drive.

"She's around the corner, like two blocks away. She's at Ray's condo," Sabrina answered.

I was happy she wasn't too far. Their brother Ray had an upscale condo that I had been to plenty of times before so I drove straight there. I was happy to see that Erykah was waiting outside for us because I would've been pissed if I would've had to wait on her. There was never parking in the area and it would've just been a frustrating ordeal.

"What's up, birthday girl?" Erykah said as soon as she got in the car.

"Hey. I haven't seen you in so long. How have you been?" I quizzed looking through the rearview mirror at Erykah as I spoke.

"Not as good as you," she said with a chortle. "You went and lucked up on a nigga like Romelo."

I let out a nervous laugh because the way she said it sounded like she was a bit jealous. "I know, right? But, I love him. That's my baby," I said so she would know that he was off limits. Erykah had never done any sheisty shit, like steal a boyfriend from me before but she had done it to others in the past, including one of her own cousins.

"Love? You love him already?" I heard Sabrina ask.

"Yes," I said sticking true to how I felt. "He told me last night when we were at dinner."

"Y'all moving fast as hell," Erykah said. "How long y'all been together?"

I shrugged. "Three weeks or so. I don't know, but I've never felt like this before."

"Wow! I need a love like that," Erykah added.

I didn't say anything else, but I did notice Sabrina giving Erykah the side eye.

We went to find something to wear in Neiman Marcus. I settled on a black and white Alexander McQueen dress that was the most expensive dress that I owned. It retailed for $2325. It was only right that I got a pair of Christian Louboutin sandals to go with it. After shopping, I dropped Leilani off at home so she could get dressed before I went around the corner to Sabrina's apartment. I fixed Sabrina's hair as best as I could in her kitchen. By the time I was finished, it was around 8:35 and I still had to get myself home and dressed. Just as I was gathering my things with my phone in my hand, it rang. I was trying to swing my bag over my shoulder while trying to answer it at the same time. "Hello?"

"So, you're going to this party tonight but you not even going to stop by to say hi to your mother on your birthday?" my mom asked.

"I'm sorry. I really been ripping and running all day long," I replied.

"Well, you better be over here within a week at least and call your dad. He said he called you earlier but you didn't bother to pick up your phone," my mother added.

"Okay, I will, but I gotta go, Mom. I told Romelo that I'd be home by nine and I'm still at Sabrina's," I said, waving bye to Sabrina and Erykah.

"Okay, but I need to meet this nigga soon, especially since you've been staying with him. But I'm not going to hold you up. Just bring him with you when you come by the house."

"Alright, ma, I got you. Love you, Ladybug."

"Love you too. Have fun tonight."

ROMELO

I was waiting for Jenae to get home since she said would be here by nine but she didn't actually get home until closer to 9:20. I was on the edge 'cause it was about to be a big night for me, well us, since she was going to be by my side.

"You found something to wear?" I asked as I followed her up the stairs.

"Yeah," she turned around to face me as she walked up the steps backward. "I got this sexy ass black dress."

"Nae, be careful because if you fall, I'm gonna laugh at you," I told her.

"I'm good," Jenae said and she was. She walked right up the stairs and into the bedroom.

"You right," I followed her into the room and a huge smile spread across my face because she stopped dead in her tracks when she saw what I had placed on it for her.

Jenae spun around her hands on her face and tears in her eyes. "Babe, you didn't."

"You said that you wanted to get back started on YouTube so I got all your shit for you," I explained.

I'd gone to the Best Buy after I dropped lunch off to her and picked up a new MacBook Pro, an iMac computer, and a Canon T3 Rebel camera. "I even got the tripod. I got all the shit that the guy in the store said that you needed for a YouTube channel. Oh, and I ordered you a… ummm… circle light."

"A ring light?" Jenae cut in, eyes wide.

"Yeah, a ring light. It'll be here in a few days. You can use the bedroom in the back to set up," I explained.

She wrapped her arms around my neck before she began kissing me passionately. "Thank you so much, babe. You really got everything I needed. Thank you."

"You're welcome," I replied. "Now, get dressed." I attempted to wait in our bedroom as Jenae took her shower, but I decided it would be great to conserve water. So, I got in the shower with her.

"You know we'll be late if you get in the shower with me," Jenae said.

I didn't say anything. I just kissed her on the neck.

"Melo," she whined. "My hair is going to get messed up." Jenae had on a scarf and a shower cap so I doubted that was true, which is why I continued to kiss her neck before I slipped my hand between her legs.

She dropped her head back in ecstasy, allowing me to continue. I knew that sex in the shower would leave her wanting more because it did so, often. I stepped out the shower, dripping wet. I didn't need to tell Jenae to follow me. She already knew what the deal was.

She bent her ass over the sink with a leg up on the counter where I slid in from behind. That shower cap wasn't going to do it for me. I needed to hold onto her hair, so I took it off. Jenae was too into it to complain. I pulled her hair while I hit it from behind, all while Jenae threw that phat ass back. I watched it as it bounced each time it collided with me.

"You like this dick, Nae?"

"Ooh yes, Melo, you know I love your dick. You know I love the way you feel when you're in me."

Just hearing her talk dirty to me, had me on the verge of nutting in her. "I'm about to cum. Where you want me to put it?"

"Ooh, cum in me," Jenae said and I did just that. With two last deep strokes, I was dropping all my seeds in her pussy.

When I pulled out, Jenae took her leg off the counter and asked, "Now can I shower in peace?"

"If you have to, unless you want a round two," I

said before smacking her on the ass.

"No, cause then we're going to be late."

"I could never be late to my own club, love. The party doesn't start until I arrive."

"You're so damn cocky. But, no, I'm more than good," Jenae said as she tried to get her scarf situated but my dick was rising again at the sight of her body.

I began to stroke myself. Jenae glanced down at it then back up at me. "Oh, no you don't I'm not about to—"

I shut her up by kissing her. I picked Jenae up and she wrapped her legs around my waist before I sat her on the counter and slid back into my favorite spot on earth.

"Ooh, babe. I hate you, right now," she moaned but had to stop talking when I started kissing her again.

"I love you," I said as I slowly pumped in and out of her.

"Fuck, I love you too, Melo," she said before she dropped her head back as she came on my dick.

I could feel her walls clenching around me, causing me to cum inside of her. I pulled out, kissed her on the cheek before getting back into the shower.

Jenae however, was still on the sink, trying to catch her breath.

"Girl, you're okay. Come and get in the shower," I said as I watched her.

"I don't even think my legs work," she complained.

"Do you need me to come get you? I can carry you if you want."

Jenae vigorously shook her head from side to side. "Nah, 'cause you're going to try to put that thing back inside of me." She hopped up and joined me in the shower. I kept my hands off her, otherwise, we would have never gotten out of there.

It didn't take me anytime to get dressed so I spent most of the time watching Jenae.

"Why you staring at me like that?" she asked me as she fixed her baby hair in the mirror.

"Like what?" I queried.

"I don't know. You're just staring at me. What's up?" she asked again.

"I'm just taking a moment to admire what's mine," I confessed.

"What's yours? You make it sound like I'm a

piece of property."

"Nah. Never that. I'm just happy to have you in my life. I want you in my life for the rest of my life," I said causing Jenae to put her little brush down and turn all the way around to face me, instead of looking at me through the mirror.

"You talking about the rest of your life as if we didn't just meet three weeks ago," she said with a nervous smile on her face.

"So, you're telling me that you don't feel the same way?" I asked nervous that she didn't feel the same way about me that I felt about her.

"I do and it's just crazy as hell to me. I've never felt like this before."

"If you feel the same way, marry me," I demanded.

Jenae's eyes bucked. "Nigga, you lying."

I turned around and picked up the ring that I'd place on my dresser earlier that day. "I'm dead serious, Nae." I walked over to her and got down on one knee before opening the box to reveal the ring. "Jenae Marie Thomas, will you marry a nigga?"

"Yes. Of course," she responded. Jenae was holding back tears trying not to mess up her makeup.

I stood up and put that big ass ring on her finger before we shared an intimate kiss.

7 CHAPTER NAME

JENAE

I wanted to pinch myself because it couldn't possibly be real life. I was with Mike for years and he never mentioned marriage or our future. But, I guess when you find that right person you just know. Mike was never my soulmate but Romelo, he truly was. We connected on a spiritual level. I didn't care what other people may have had to say about how fast we were moving either.

I pulled my lips away from Romelo's and said, "Can we get to this party now?"

"Yeah, but I got one more surprise for you."

"What? How?" I quizzed. "I feel like you've done enough already."

"Nah, get used to this. I plan on spoiling you. You ready? The surprise is at the club," he replied.

"Yeah. Just let me put my shoes on," I slipped my feet back into my pumps, grabbed my clutch and was ready to walk out the door. But first, I stopped and took a picture of myself in front of the mirror. You could see Romelo in the background. Any other time, I would have cropped him out, but I was riding high, so I posted it to Instagram and tagged him with the caption: *Just know, this is officially the best birthday I've ever had.*

I knew we were late because, by the time Romelo and I got to Power, Sabrina, Justin, Tracee, Erykah, and Leilani were sitting up at a table in VIP. "Hey, y'all." I waved with my left hand so that they could see my new ring.

Tracee was the first one to spot it. "That's not what I think it is, is it?"

I tossed my hair over my shoulder with my left hand, still showing off the ring. "That depends on what you think."

"Is it a promise ring, like when Mike gave you one?" Erykah asked.

I cut my eyes at her and was about to speak but Romelo did first. "Nah, sweetheart. It's an engagement ring. I asked Jenae to marry me."

Sabrina and Leilani got up and rushed me. "Oh, my goodness. Congratulations!" Sabrina exclaimed.

"Thank you," I said blushing while I spoke. I gave them both a hug before I went to take a seat on the red velvet bench.

Romelo came and whispered in my ear, "I'll be right back. I gotta go check on a few things."

"Okay," I said before he kissed me on the cheek and walked off with Justin in tow.

"Y'all engaged already? You pregnant?" Erykah quizzed.

"No. He just knows what he wants and I feel the same way," I said.

"Wow. That's crazy," Erykah said but not once did she say congratulations. She just had a salty look on her face. I didn't feed into it though and no one else even noticed.

"You want a drink?" Tracee asked trying to relieve some of the mounting tension.

"I guess. I'm not driving tonight, so it's fine," I replied. Tracee started making me a drink of Ciroc and cranberry juice but stopped suddenly like she'd seen a ghost. "What's wrong?" I asked looking over in the direction where Tracee was staring. I saw Black walking up to the VIP, alongside Romelo and some other guy I'd never laid eyes on.

The one I didn't know walked over and kissed my little sister on the lips. That must've been Keraun. Seeing them together almost made me forget that Black was walking up on Tracee, but the look of anger on his face wouldn't let me. I watched as he whispered in Tracee's ear. Without hesitation, she got up and followed him out the VIP. Something told me that I wouldn't see either of them for the rest of the night. With Romelo next to me, I asked, "How you know Black?"

"Oh, that's the homie. He's the head of security here. Why?" Romelo asked.

"Cause he's Tracee's baby father. I don't think she knew he would be here. From the looks of it, I don't even think she knew he worked here. I just hope don't nothing jump off 'cause knowing them, it was certainly a possibility."

"If it does, that's between them. Now focus on having a good time," Romelo said before kissing me softly on the neck.

The party was lit but I was too wrapped up in my

man to actually care. When people found out that Romelo was single there were a lot of chicks that thought they stood a chance but that wasn't the case. Them seeing me on his arm on me all night had a few onlookers red hot. One chick even went as far as to post about it on her Instagram story and tagged the club's location in it. When Sabrina was browsing the stories from the night, she showed it to me as we shared a good laugh. As long as they didn't do or say anything to me personally, I didn't care.

"I've got to use the bathroom. You coming with me?" Sabrina asked me over the music.

"Yeah," I stood up to follow her and all the other ladies did so as well. We followed each other in a close line to the bathroom, making sure we didn't get separated along the way.

I didn't actually need to pee and once we made it through the line I stood at the mirror and touched up my makeup. Erykah locked the door to the bathroom while Sabrina and Leilani went into separate stalls.

"Why you lock the bathroom door, like that? I'm not using the bathroom, so someone else can come in," I said.

"Because I don't need those hoes all up in my business," Erykah said as she pulled out a little baggy of coke.

"You still doing that stuff?" I quizzed.

"Only when I'm out. It's not that often, but I gotta make tonight fun since y'all all booed up."

It wasn't my thing to do coke. Sabrina tried it once at the urging of her big sister but ultimately, she decided that it wasn't for her. It was a good thing too. I certainly didn't want a cokehead for a best friend.

Erykah only did a bump of coke and was cleaned up before Sabina or Leilani emerged from the bathroom. Sabrina gave Erykah the side eye as if she knew exactly what her sister was up to, but Leilani was oblivious.

"Are we going to breakfast of anything after this?" Leilani quizzed as she washed her hands.

"I'm not sure what's happening after this, but you better introduce me to Keraun before the night is over," I said.

"Of course," Leilani replied.

"Come on. Erykah, you done?" Sabrina quizzed as we walked over to the door.

I watched as Erykah held onto her nose, trying my best not to make a face in disgust. I exited the bathroom and was headed back to the VIP when my eyes locked on Alyssa's. Half of me wanted her to say something to me, but the other half didn't really want any drama to pop off.

Alyssa didn't say anything as I walked by. I went to sit next to Romelo but he pulled me into his lap, wrapping his arms around my waist. He was planting kisses all over my neck when I noticed Alyssa was standing directly in front of us, hands on her hips and anger on her face. I stared her down with a smile on my face, daring her to speak.

She waited until all eyes were on her before she spoke. "So, you give this bitch the same ring you gave me? Let me find out that you're too broke to get a new ring."

I looked down at my engagement ring before standing up. My left hand was my dominant hand and I didn't like the idea of getting blood on my ring so my right hand would have to suffice when I punched that bitch in the face. I was gearing up to do so when Romelo stood up and got in front of me.

"Fuck you even here for? You know I never gave you a fucking ring. You just came to start shit, like you ain't get ya shit knocked in that last time you approached her. Where the fuck is the damn secur—"

Romelo stopped talking once he saw that Leilani had the hoe by the hair and had taken it upon herself to escort Alyssa out the VIP section. Our daddy ain't raise no punks and my little sister rode hard as hell for me, no questions asked. Keraun was trying to stop her while I was being held back, by Romelo.

"Lani, chill," I could hear Keraun saying but that girl wasn't listening. She was on a mission. Security finally arrived and escorted Alyssa out the building.

"Who the fuck was that?" Leilani finally asked me.

"The ex that obviously can't let go," I said taking a seat before fixing myself a new drink.

Romelo took a seat next to me, rubbed my thigh and asked, "You good?"

"I'm fine. You okay? She tried you, just now," I said.

He laughed just a little. "Yeah. I'm straight, especially since I got you by my side."

I blushed before I gave him a kiss on the lips. "I love you."

"I love you too. Now let's turn the fuck up."

"You ain't said nothing but a word." I drank my drink before I pulled Romelo up so that he could dance with me. As soon as Future's song Mask Off came on I moved my hips to the beat while my ass was pressed up against him.

When the song ended Romelo turned me around and looked and me and said, "Remember that surprise I have for you? It's time."

"Melo," I groaned. "I think you did enough already." I didn't want to sound ungrateful, but I wasn't used to someone doing so much for me. It was overwhelming.

"Just follow me outside," Romelo said taking me by the hand.

I wasn't sure if everyone was in on it or not, but Sabrina, Leilani, Justin, Keraun, and Erykah all followed us outside. Tracee had ventured off somewhere with Black so she wasn't with us as Romelo took me out to the parking lot. A crowd was forming when I noticed what was sitting before me with a big red bow was the fanciest car that I'd ever laid my eyes on. I looked over at Romelo and he had the key in his hand, dangling them on his index finger.

I hesitated before I took the key. "This is mine?"

"Who else would it be for? Of course, it's for you," Romelo assured me.

"Babe," I said as I was fanning myself to keep from crying. "You didn't have to do all of this."

ERYKAH

You ever see something happening and just can't believe your damn eyes? That was me. It was hard watching this fairy tale shit happen to Jenae. Don't get me wrong. I loved her like a little sister, but Romelo literally fell into her lap and from the looks of things, she didn't even know how to handle a nigga like him.

Romelo seemed to love everything about her. He even put a ring on it in less than a month. In the meantime, I was single as hell and occasionally getting dick from Cisco, my sister's ex. I didn't even like Cisco, but I had bills to pay and he was generous. Why Sabrina let that nigga go, I would never understand because the sex was out of this world.

I watched as Jenae got into her new car, before getting right back out to kiss Romelo. He had a cocky ass smile, but he had every reason to be cocky. That nigga was everything in the city of Baltimore. I couldn't take any more of the mushy shit, so I slipped back into the club. When I walked in I could've sworn that I saw Cisco out the corner of my eye. I just prayed that he hadn't seen me because the last thing I needed was him to come over and blow up my spot.

I wasn't the only one in the section when I

returned but I was the only one from our table. I made a drink and was on my second one when I heard someone calling my name. I looked up from my phone to see Cisco. I walked over to him and said, "What's up?"

"You here alone?" He pulled me close to him. So close, that I was able to smell the Hennessey on his breath.

I backed up before I spoke. "No, I'm here with Sabrina and Jenae. They're probably on their way back over here so you need to back up."

"Why you nervous?" Cisco asked, invading my space again.

"Because my sister and her best friend are here. I'm not trying to have that type of drama happen tonight," I replied as I put some distance between us for the second time.

"You still not ready to tell her about us?"

I laughed in Cisco's face at the question. "There is no us. Not when you're still texting Sabrina telling her that you want her back."

It was Cisco's turn to laugh because I knew what he'd been up to. "Man, that ain't really mean shit. You know you're the one I want."

"Whatever. I'm not about to start beefing with my

sister because of you," I explained but that was too late.

I heard someone clear their throat and when I turned my head in the direction of the noise. I was face to face with my little sister. Cisco had his hand on the small of my back and I was clearly busted. "Sabrina."

"Erykah, it's cool. I always knew you liked him and I've moved on. But Francisco, I hope this means you'll stop calling my phone, begging for another chance." Sabrina walked off and sat next to Jenae. I didn't know what was said, but from the look of disgust on Jenae's face, I knew it wasn't good.

"So now she knows," Cisco said forcing me to look at him.

"Fuck you, Cisco," I said walking off. I went and got my clutch from where I'd been sitting so I could leave, calling an Uber on my way out the door.

SABRINA

Nothing surprises me about Erykah anymore. I love her and I tolerate her because she is my big sister. She stepped up to the plate when our alcoholic mother was too busy chasing dick to be bothered with us. But we were grown now and Erykah always acted like I owed her something.

She did have to grow up fast, which is why I overlooked so many of her flaws but I thought she knew Cisco was off limits. Not even that he was mine but she watched the nigga dog my ass out. Erykah was one of the shoulders that I cried on just for her to turn around and start fucking him. That cut me real deep.

"Man, fuck Erykah. She'll get what's coming to her, dealing with a nigga like Cisco. He's only out for self," Jenae said trying to make me feel better.

"I know. He's just doing the shit to get under my skin because I curved his ass but Erykah's too dumb to see that shit. That's 'cause she still snorting that shit," I said. My entire night was ruined and nothing anyone said or did was going to make me feel better.

"I'm sorry you had to see that, though," Jenae said.

"Right. I'm going to head out now too. Happy Birthday, boo! I'll call you tomorrow," I said before I went to find Justin to let him know I was leaving. I'd driven my car with Erykah so he wouldn't be forced to end his night early on account of me being in my feelings.

"You okay?" Justin asked as soon as he saw my face.

"Erykah just did some foul shit. I need to cut out early."

"You want me to come with you?" he asked.

"No. You don't have to. I kind of just want to be alone," I told him.

"Okay, but I'm gonna walk you out to your car."

I didn't object to Justin walking me out to the car because Cisco could've been lurking somewhere and the last thing I wanted to do was talk to him.

"Call me as soon as you get home," Justin said as I got in the car.

"Okay, babe. Have fun. Don't let my leaving ruin your night," I replied.

"No, you ain't ruin nothing," Justin said before flashing his megawatt smile.

That got me smiling before I drove home. On my way, I heard my phone buzz. It was sitting in the passenger seat, face up. When I glanced at it there was a text message from Erykah. She'd sent a damn essay. I wasn't going to read it while I was driving. I wasn't even sure if I wanted to read it at all. Once I was in the house, shoes off and a glass of wine in my hand, I surprised myself by reading the message.

Erykah: *Bree, I'm so sorry you had to find out about me talking to Francisco like that. That was never my intention. It's not that deep with him and before you go jumping to conclusions, I wasn't fucking with him while y'all were together. I ran into him a few months ago at a bar and we were both drunk. I know that's really no excuse. I've just been in a tight spot and he's been helping me out with rent and my bills. I hope you don't stay mad at me for too long. Love you, sissy.*

There was no way that I could bring myself to respond to her damn text message. All Erykah ever did was make excuses for her own fucked up decisions. I wasn't going to cut her off, but I needed some time to get over it.

CHAPTER EIGHT

ROMELO

Jenae jumped in her car with her little sister and I followed in mine behind her. We were headed to breakfast because she was still geeked about the entire night. Only Keraun and Leilani were coming along, though.

"Do you see how much that shit sparkles, though?" Jenae asked Leilani as we sat at our table waiting for our waitress to come.

"Yes. You shinin', shinin', shinin', shinin', yeah," Leilani sang.

"All of this winning," Jenae added the next line before she started laughing. "So, Mr. Keraun. Who are you?"

I looked over at my fiancée wondering where she was going with that line of questioning. "He good peoples, babe."

"I believe you," Jenae replied. "But, I don't know him and that's my little sister."

"You don't see her questioning me like crazy. Let Lani live," I said.

"It's cool. Lani warned me that you were gonna ask a bunch of questions," Keraun interjected being a good sport.

"Good. You're friends with Melo, so I doubt you're broke. I'm not gon' ask you what it is you do because I doubt you'd tell me the truth anyway." Jenae clearly didn't have a filter when she was in big sister mode. "So, do you have any kids?"

I almost spit out my mouth full of orange juice when she asked that. Keraun had three kids and possibly two on the way.

"Yeah," he replied.

Leilani looked pissed when kids were brought up but Jenae didn't notice her face. Keraun must've told Leilani about slipping up with his baby mom, Paris, and getting her pregnant.

"By how many women?" Jenae quizzed.

"One," Leilani said forcing a smile before she added, "She's nice."

"That's good," Jenae replied. "I'm not going to get all up in your business since Romelo can vouch for you. But, I will say this, if you break my little sister's heart, I'll break your legs." After she said that gangsta shit, a smile spread across her lips.

"Well the same goes for you, Romelo," Leilani said pointing at me.

"You ain't got shit to worry about over here," I assured her before I squeezed Jenae's thigh underneath the table.

She looked up at me with a smile on her face before mouthing, "I love you."

"I love you, too," I mouthed back.

"Yo, y'all niggas is sickening," Keraun said before laughing. "When you get so damn mushy?"

"Don't hate," Jenae said before sticking her tongue out.

"Yo, you and Lani act just alike," he replied laughing while our girls both nodded their heads.

I'd never been on a double date, done any PDA or any shit that niggas did on TV, but I also never had a girl like Jenae. Her energy was infectious. Positive vibes were rubbing off on me like a motherfucker. After breakfast, we met back up at the house and didn't even make it all the way upstairs before we tore each other's clothes off. I knew that I'd made Jenae's birthday special and in turn, she showed me just how grateful she truly was.

In the morning, I woke up and Jenae wasn't in the bed with me. I got out of bed and threw on a pair of sweatpants and went downstairs. It was my turn to be surprised. At the front of the living room, there were balloons that said, "Happy G-Day Melo." I had to laugh at that. I'd only seen those balloons on Instagram. They were big as hell and I was surprised that she managed to get them in the house without me knowing.

I headed to the kitchen because Jenae wasn't in the living room. I stood in the doorway, just watching her. She was at the stove in a pair of black short shorts and a grey Calvin Klein sports bra, looking sexy, while singing The Sweetest Thing by Lauryn Hill, acapella. I could stand there and watch her all day. Jenae's voice was so clear and soulful. I was a little upset when she stopped singing because she noticed me.

Jenae gasped and her hand flew to her chest. "You scared me. How long were you even standing there?"

"Not long," I replied as I walked over to her. "What you in here cooking?"

"French toast, eggs, and bacon. I just knew I was going to bring this to you in the bed. Why did you wake up so early? I didn't put it on you well enough last night, then," Jenae looked at me, upset with her hands on her hips.

"So, you want me to get back in the bed?" I quizzed.

"No. We can eat over here at the table," she said gesturing towards the kitchen table.

"Okay," I took a seat at the table. Jenae continued to cook breakfast, while I snapped pictures. Once I got one that looked perfect, I posted it to Instagram with the caption:

All a nigga need as a birthday gift is this woman right here. #MyFutureWife #YouReadThatRight #ANiggaAsked #SheSaidYes

Then I tagged her in the post.

As Jenae sat our meals on the table she asked, "Why are you cheesing so damn hard?"

"'Cause you make a nigga happy. After breakfast,

I gotta make a quick run, okay."

"A run. I had something planned. I wanted to celebrate your birthday right since you made mine perfect.

"I won't be too long. I gotta pick something up. What you got planned?"

"It's a surprise, but I need you to back a bag and be pack here no later than noon."

JUSTIN

"Open the door. I'm outside," I said into the phone to Sabrina.

A few moments passed before she swung the door open. Her eyes looked like they were puffy as if she'd been crying all night.

"I thought I told you that I wanted to be alone," Sabrina said as she still stepped to the side to let me in.

"Nah, I left you alone last night, but you not about to spend the day crying over some nigga." I took a seat on the couch.

"I wasn't crying all day and it wasn't because of Cisco. It was because of Erykah," she explained.

"Well, tell me the situation because what I heard so far ain't good," I said to her.

"I'm not sure what you heard or even where you could have heard it, but Erykah is fucking my ex."

"So, why you upset?" I asked not seeing a reason for the tears. "You still want the nigga or something?"

"No, I just feel disrespectful by my sister."

"But, if you don't want the nigga and y'all not still

fucking, why are you all in your feelings about it? Let Erykah do what she wants."

"So, you wouldn't feel some type of way if your brothers started messing with your ex," Sabrina quizzed.

"Nah, cause if she's my ex, then she's my ex for a reason."

"Meaning if you and I break up, you wouldn't be mad with me if I started fucking one of them?" she asked, trying to get me to change my mind.

"It's not that big of a deal, Sabrina. Now get dressed. A nigga hungry and I wanted to get some breakfast before you gotta go to work."

She stood up and sucked her teeth. "The only reason you wouldn't feel a way is because you're a nigga, but Erykah violated girl code."

"Y'all girls always talking about girl code, but maybe you should just worry about yourself. You know how Erykah is and the nigga did you dirty in the past. You can't expect more from people than they're able to give. That's how you set yourself up for failure."

Sabrina sighed before she said, "You're right. That shit just threw me off." I watched her as she wiped away the tears that were beginning to form.

"You gotta work today?" I asked.

"Yeah. I close tonight. I was just about to get dressed. What are you doing tonight?"

"I'm heading in the club for a bit. I got some shit to take care of for Melo with Rashad. I'll pick you up from work." I stood up so that I could leave and Sabrina stood up as well.

"Can I get a kiss before you go?"

"Of course," I said before I planted a kiss on her lips and gave a quick squeeze to her ass. I wasn't trying to get anything started but the way that she pressed her body against mine told me all I needed to know.

I lifted Sabrina up and wrapped her legs around my waist. I carried her to the bedroom all while tonguing her down. I dropped her down onto the bed and climbed on top of her while she started to pull my shirt over my head. We both had things to do for the day so I decided on a quickie. I stuck my hands into her pajamas shorts and was pleasantly surprised by the fact that she wasn't wearing any panties. After rubbing her clit for a bit, I pulled them down with one hand and unbuckled my pants with the other.

Sabrina was good and wet when I slid into her. She was propped up on her elbows and once I was all the way inside, she dropped her head back and moaned in ecstasy. "Oooh, baby."

"You like this?" I asked as I gave her deep slow strokes.

"Fuck yes, Justin. I can feel you in my stomach," Sabrina replied as her hand went to her stomach.

With each stroke, I was going as deep as I could go and Sabrina was throwing that shit back at me. I started thinking about hockey and baseball. Shit, anything to keep from nutting fast as hell but Sabrina started to twist her hips and tighten her pussy around my dick, causing me to coat her walls with my seed.

"Damn, you know how I feel about you doing all that extra shit," I said when I pulled out.

"I couldn't help myself. It felt so fucking good," Sabrina said standing up with me. "But I came and so did you, so that's all that matters. I'm going to take a shower, now."

"Let me join you."

LEILANI

"So, if she's pregnant what does that mean for us?" I asked Keraun. He'd told me the day before Paris being pregnant, but I need a moment to take it in before I could have a real conversation with him about it. I was putting on a front in front of my big sister about being upset that he'd gotten his baby mom pregnant but truth be told I was pissed and hurt.

Keraun had the nerve to shrug. "It's all in your hands."

"Bad enough you had three kids when we met. I couldn't be mad at that but this is different. And for her to know me and smile in my face while knowing that y'all were still fucking if the crazy part."

"We weren't still fucking. You making it sound like it was a regular thing. It happened one time," Keraun interjected.

"One time is enough. How far along is she? Should the two of us have a conversation? Do you want to be with her now?" My insecurities were getting the best of me and I was getting frustrated because I was on the brink of tears but I didn't want to cry in front of him. I wanted to appear strong but truth be told, I wasn't.

"As long as you don't plan on putting your hands on her, y'all can have all the conversations you see fit. She said that she feels bad because she likes you."

I flagged him. Who gave a fuck if the baby mom still like me if she was still fucking my man? I sure didn't. "I just know how dumb I'll look when my sister finds out. Does Melo know?"

"Yeah."

"Fuck, then that means that Jenae is gonna find out soon too," I said irritated because I wanted my sister to hear it straight from me.

"He's not going to tell her anything. Calm down. You're getting yourself worked up but we don't even know if they're mine and I'm not going anywhere," Keraun said trying to reassure me.

"You may not be going anywhere but I refuse for this to be some kind of harem. If you're with me you're only with me. Don't go backsliding with her again. Don't take my forgiveness this time as a sign of weakness."

"I'm not. You know, I love you."

I was standing between his legs and when he said that he loved me, I looked down at him and into his eyes and said, "Don't say those words if you don't mean them."

He wrapped his hands around my waist and said, "You know that I don't say things I don't mean. I don't throw that word around, but I really love you, Leilani."

"I love you too." When those words left my mouth, Keraun pulled me in close for a kiss.

"So, you gonna ride with ya nigga?" he quizzed once our lips parted.

"Of course. But now I gotta go write this paper because it's due by midnight and I didn't even start it." I was in my senior year of college and in my last semester, less than a month from graduation. I needed to make sure that I didn't do anything that would prevent me from getting my degree in History because since I was a little girl, I wanted to be a History Teacher.

"Well, you better get on it, then," Keraun said before he hit me on my ass. I stuck out my tongue before I headed up to his bedroom where my laptop and backpack were waiting for me.

CHAPTER NINE

JENAE

"Where are you taking me?" Romelo asked me for the fourth time in the past half hour.

"Can you just be quiet and let me drive?" I quizzed.

"Okay, but I got one last question. Are we getting on a plane, or just driving out there?" he asked me.

"We're getting on a flight, which is why we're headed to the airport. Now can you stop asking questions? And before you tell me that you can't go away because of work, I told Antonio and Justin that we were going out of town and to be you until you get back."

"So, you really planned this shit all the way out?" Romelo asked with a smile on his face.

"Yes. Now, sit back, relax, and enjoy the ride."

I parked in the airport parking lot before taking a shuttle to the departure gate for American Airlines. I used a kiosk and checked us in with Romelo peering over my shoulder. "Can you back up?"

"I'm trying to see where this plane is taking us."

"Nooo," I whined. "It's a surprise. Don't ruin it."

"Okay," he finally said, giving in.

I printed our boarding passes and we went through security check and finally to our gate where he was able to see that we were on our way to Las Vegas.

"You booked us a trip to Vegas. You trying to get married out there," he asked as we took a seat before our flight began boarding.

"No!" I hit him playfully. "I like going away for my birthday. Normally I'd go somewhere with Bree but between her working like crazy and the fact that your birthday is the day after mine, I thought this was more fitting. You ready to turn up?"

"That depends," he replied throwing me for a bit of a loop.

"It depends on what?" I queried with an eyebrow raised, awaiting his reply.

"On where you got a nigga staying. I mean, I know you ain't got that much money."

I put my hand up to stop him from finishing that statement. "I have a good room. I know how to book a trip babe. Just have some faith in me, please. Otherwise, you won't get to see me in my new bikini."

Romelo licked his thick lips and said, "Okay. So, I'm going to keep my mouth shut then."

"Good." I smiled before Romelo kissed me on the lips. I may have gotten him to shut his mouth but he'd made me nervous. I wasn't sure if my trip would be up to his standards.

I'd booked a room for us at the Aria Hotel on the strip. I had tickets to a pool party that would be taking place over the weekend. However, the main point of the trip was to take him shopping. Yes, this was something he could do on his own, but I wanted to try to spoil him the same way he'd been spoiling me. If that meant dipping into my savings to do it, then that's what I was going to do.

As soon as we touched down, I picked up our rental car from Enterprise. It was a Chrysler 200 and as soon as the guy assisting me pulled it up, Romelo said, "Oh hell no. What is this?"

"Babe it's the only car I could really afford since they charge me more for being under twenty-five," I admitted.

"Aya, homie. Can we just cancel this car? I'm gonna try to get something else," Romelo said just as the guy was bringing over the keys.

"Is there something wrong with the car?" the Enterprise employee quizzed.

"Nah, it's just not my speed. Thank you, though," Romelo replied, grabbed my hand and led me away.

"So, what are we supposed to do now? We don't have a car." I was beyond irritated but I was trying my best to keep my tone neutral.

"I'm going to find a car for us, but I can't ride around in that basic shit." Romelo pulled out his phone and made a call. I couldn't quite make out what he was saying, but while he spoke, he took me by the hand and led me away.

I didn't say anything because I wasn't sure what was even going on. I just followed him out to the ride share pick up location. From there we took an Uber to a car rental place called Exotic Car Collection. It was a part of the Enterprise company but they had cars I couldn't possibly afford to own, at least not without the assistance of Romelo. My stomach dropped when I saw that damn white Aston Martin D89 being pulled out. I had to wipe my mouth to make sure that I wasn't drooling at the sight of it.

Once we were in the Aston Martin, Romelo asked, "What hotel are we staying at?"

"I got us a room at Aria and it's a luxury hotel, so don't go trying to make any changes to it."

"Nah, you good. I've heard good things about that place, so I'ma let you live."

"Thank you." I was low key annoyed with him and his need to be in control. Honestly, any other time it didn't bother me, but this was my trip and I was supposed to be the one running the show. "I'm glad you approve."

Romelo laughed and asked, "Yo, you feeling some type of way or something?"

"No, Melo, I don't feel any type of way that you're trying to commandeer this whole thing."

"Oh, damn. I wasn't trying to do that. Alright, I promise to let this stay your trip as much as possible," he said but we both knew that wasn't true. The next chance he got, Romelo would step in, if he thought it would make our trip better.

"Whatever," I mumbled because that was the last

thing I wanted to say on the matter.

We got the car valet parked and while I was getting checked in, Romelo couldn't help but to request an upgrade to the room, there was a difference in $1200. All of it was going on my credit card. I had the money but it was eating into what I'd put to the side to spend on Romelo for his shopping spree. It was going to end up being a small ass spree. I must say that despite the irritation about the money he'd spend, the room was worth it. I'd never stayed in a suite, but a girl could certainly get used to it.

First things first, I took a shower and since it was only four in the afternoon, I got dressed in my new bikini because I wanted to head down to the pool. I dragged my suitcase into the bathroom with me so I could have easy access to my toiletries, but I also put on my bathing suit while I was in there. It was a yellow string bikini that was up in my ass and barely covered my titties. I looked like an Instagram model and could give the model Austin Tyler a run for her money. I just knew I was going to be shitting on any other bitches that were down at the pool. However, as soon as I stepped out the bathroom and into the bedroom, the look on Romelo's face told me that he wasn't feeling my swimwear.

"Where you going in that?" he quizzed.

I did a little spin to show him the entire swimsuit.

"What's wrong with this?"

"The fact that it's smaller than the panties and bras you wear."

I sucked my teeth before saying, "That's what we're not going to do. I look cute in this, plus I'm with you so it's not like niggas about to be stepping to me," I replied.

"That's not even the point, Nae," Romelo rebuffed.

"Then tell me what the point is, Romelo," I said, hands on my hips in indignation.

"You not about to be out here showing niggas all your goodies. I'ma need you to go change."

"I'ma need you to not think that you're my daddy. I already have one of those. Let's just have a good time, please." I planned on putting on a black sheer cover-up, but that wasn't the point. I didn't like the idea that Romelo thought it would be okay to tell me what I could and couldn't wear, especially if I didn't think that what I had on was inappropriate.

"Whatever, yo. I'm not even tryna argue with you. I'm 'bout to take a shower and then we can go down to the pool."

I didn't say anything else because I didn't want to argue with him, either. I unpacked and put on my cover up with a pair of Tory Burch flip flops, in black. I took a few pictures with my phone while I waited before I pulled out my new camera and started fooling around with it. I planned on getting a bunch of use out of it during the trip.

I was out on the balcony waiting on Romelo when he finally walked out in a black t-shirt and a pair of red plaid Burberry trunks.

"You ready to go down to the pool?"

"Yeah. Just let me take your picture first," I said standing up, pointing the camera in his direction.

Romelo clasped his hands in front of him but didn't smile. I snapped a couple pictures, then looked at the display. "You look good in these."

"I always look good, Nae."

"Well then, let's go. I really want to get in the pool." I sat my camera on the dresser, grabbed my phone with the waterproof pouch and followed him out the room and down to the pool.

Romelo took a seat in one of the chairs, while I got right in the pool, no hesitation. I swam up to the side and said to him," Come get in the pool."

"Nah, I'm good."

"Nigga, I know you didn't come all the way down

here with Burberry Trunks and all, just to not get in the damn water," I groaned.

Romelo laughed but he didn't get up.

"Wait, don't tell me that you can't swim," I said assuming that had to be the case. I didn't want Romelo to be a stereotype of a black man that can't swim.

"I can swim, Nae."

"Then get in the damn pool," I insisted.

"Alright, just give me a second," Romelo said finally giving me my way.

Since my phone was in a waterproof pouch, I had my Instagram Live on and was filming him as he took off his shirt. "Damn, my nigga's fine," I said admiring his washboard abs.

"Yo, you filming me right now?" he quizzed.

"Yeah. I'm on Instagram Live, so say hi," I replied.

"Nae put the phone away."

I sucked my teeth but didn't argue. He was getting in the pool like I'd asked so I decided to enjoy his company. Romelo got in the pool and immediately pinned me up against the side of the pool, burying his face in my neck. "Melo quit it."

"What? You wanted me in the pool, didn't you?" he asked.

"Sss...stop," I stammered because Romelo was turning me on.

"You don't sound like you want me to stop," he said before he began to kiss me on my neck.

"I do or you're going to start something that we can't finish out here," I said, my voice barely above a whisper.

"But you wanted me in the pool. What else am I supposed to do if you don't want me to kiss you?"

I thought about that question for a second before I pulled away. "Race me."

"Race you?" Romelo quizzed.

"Yes." I had a huge smile on my face. "Race me from here to the other side of the pool. It'll be fun."

"All right." I was surprised that he agreed and raced me. After our race, which I won, it changed the mood for the rest of the time at the pool. We were a lot more playful and officially on the same page.

We spent about an hour and a half down at the pool before we got out, both of us starving. We headed up to the suite to get dressed. I let Romelo use the bathroom first while I responded to Sabrina's text message.

Sabrina: *So, you just go to Las Vegas and don't tell anybody?*

Me: *I asked you to do a birthday vacation with me and you couldn't get time off. So, I decided to surprise Melo. I spent so much time trying to pull it off that I forgot to tell you.*

Sabrina: *Oh, you planned the trip?*

Me: *Yeah, for his birthday.*

Sabrina: *Oh okay.*

Me: *But, how are you holding up? Have you talked to Erykah?*

Sabrina: *I'm fine and I don't on talking to her. Some things you just don't do and one of them is fucking my ex. Like who the hell does that to their own sister?*

Me: *I feel you. It sounds like you're the one that needs this vacation.*

Sabrina: *Well, give me the date and I'll put in the request for some time off.*

Me: *I say the end of July. We should go somewhere fun, like London.*

Sabrina: No, I need a beach. Let's go to Belize. I hear nothing but good things about it.

Me: It don't matter to me either way. As long as you get to go on vacation. But, I'm about to go to dinner. I'll call you later.

Sabrina: Okay. Have fun and don't come back pregnant.

Me: Bitch, you know I got birth control on deck. Ain't no babies popping out of this cat anytime soon.

Sabrina: I know that's right.

Romelo walked out of the bedroom with a towel wrapped around his waist and water glistening on his body. I looked up at him and bit my bottom lip.

"You see something you like?" he quizzed.

"You know I do, but I'm also hungry so I'm going to get showered for dinner while you get dressed. I jumped up and hurried into the bathroom before Romelo could stop me.

When I got out the shower, he was sitting on the bed with my phone in his hand. "You looking for something?" I quizzed. My phone didn't have a passcode on it because I never really saw the need for one. Therefore, I knew he was looking at something on my phone but what? I had no clue.

"Mike keeps texting you."

"Okay. He always texts me. You know that." I didn't bother to take my phone from him because I had nothing to hide, therefore, I started getting dressed.

"I texted him back," Romelo said causing me to stop dead in my tracks.

"Why?" I didn't see what reason Romelo had to text Mike back other than to cause unwanted drama.

"'Cause the nigga keeps texting. It's like he's not getting the point. I know I told you to ignore him at first, but this shit is getting ridiculous."

"I know it's ridiculous, but at the same time, I'm not trying to even go there with him or even with you right now. I just want to enjoy the trip. Is that okay with you?"

"We are enjoying the trip. You not enjoying the trip?" he asked putting the phone down on the bed.

"I'm not sure, right now," I replied.

Romelo came and walked up on me. "You want me to make it better?"

I knew exactly how he planned on making it better, just by the look in his eyes. "Umm, if you think you can."

KERAUN

Paris handed me the ultrasound of what was supposed to be our twins. "You found out your due date for sure?"

"Yeah. The bloodwork came back. I'm twelve weeks along and due October 14th," she replied.

"Oh, alright," I said as I studied the ultrasound photo as if I were going to be able to tell this early whether or not the babies were mine. "Leilani wants to know if y'all can meet up."

Paris' jaw dropped. "You staying with her?"

"You thought otherwise? I fucked up once and it's not going to happen again."

Paris started to fight back tears. "So, you really want to be with that little ass girl?"

"I'm with her, ain't I? Me being with her will not stop what I can do for you and our kids. We're not getting back together because we broke up for a reason."

"You're acting like you broke up with me. We ended things because your black ass kept cheating on me. I'm ready to take you back and all you can say is that you want to be with some little young bitch."

With that, I stood up. "I'm not going to argue back and forth with you about being with my girlfriend. It's not always about Paris. I'm out."

"Baby, please don't go." Paris grabbed onto my arm in an attempt to get me to stay, but that wasn't where my head was at. When Paris and I were together, I didn't like the man I was. I did a lot of shit out of spite because she didn't trust me. When she broke up with me, I was happy since that was something I would've never done since we had kids together. The sad truth was if Paris would've never kicked me out the house, I would've still been playing games.

It wasn't that I didn't love her, but I didn't know how to love her the way she needed to be loved. Paris and I were young as hell when we got together and neither of us knew what we were really getting ourselves into. I was honestly a lot happier once I didn't have to hear Paris telling me how much I'd fucked up.

"So, it's really just fuck me now?" Paris yelled once I'd gotten my arm freed.

"Stop being dramatic. I'll swing through on Friday to pick up the kids."

"Not if you're going to have them around that bitch, Keraun," Paris said.

I turned around and with a snarl, I said, "You don't want to do that. Don't make me fuck you up because you want to play little childish games."

"You gonna fuck me up now? You hitting women now, Keraun?" Paris asked. I knew that she was trying to get me to react, but nothing that she said or did was going to make me change my mind about not wanting to be with her.

"Like I said, quit trying to play these childish ass games. You gonna fuck around and not like the outcome. I'll get the kids on Friday."

I left out the house and called Romelo. I needed him to calm me down before I went back in that house and fucked Paris' simple ass. "Yo, bro. Where you at?"

"I'm out in Vegas with Nae. What's up?" Romelo replied.

I forgot that Lani said her sister took Romelo to Vegas for his birthday. "Oh shit. I knew that."

"What's wrong, though?" he asked.

"Dealing with Paris dumb ass 'bout to make me smack the shit out of her. I'm 'bout to go get a drink, see some strippers, or some shit."

"Do what you gotta go. Just don't do no off the wall shit and remember you got a good girl waiting for you at home," Romelo said giving me some sound advice.

"You right. I'm gonna take my ass home. I'm not gonna let Paris dumb ass get to me."

ALYSSA

"Do you remember the password to that Instagram page you made so I could see if Romelo was cheating on me?" I asked Courtney.

"Yeah. I use it when I'm on those gossip blogs so I can comment without people seeing me," she answered me.

"Well, what is it?" I asked.

"What you need it for?" Courtney asked looking away from her and at me.

"Because I want to see his new bitch's page."

"Why? Don't do that to yourself.

"Whose side are you on right now?"

"You do realize that Romelo's my cousin, right?"

"But his new girl isn't your cousin and I want to see her page."

"Well, I follow her already and you're just going to make yourself upset if you try to see her page."

"How would that happen?" I asked frustrated that I wasn't getting the response from my so-called friend, that I wanted.

"Because the two of them are really happy. You saw the ring he got her."

"It's not an engagement ring, is it? No, right? He can't be engaged to that girl already. That's just not possible. They barely know each other, unless you know something that I don't. He been fucking her all along, hasn't he?"

"I'm not obligated to tell you anything. You need to be happy. I'm letting you stay here."

"I pay rent," I replied, in my feelings by her response.

"Yes, but if Melo knew you were staying here, he'd be pissed. Anyway, yes. They're engaged. Rashad told me that he asked her right before that party where homegirl gripped your ass up. They really did just meet and they're really in love. There's nothing more to even say about it either."

"How he just propose to her after less than a month but never even talked about marriage with me after all the years we were together. I did everything under the sun to keep that man and some random bitch just gets him?" I was angry as hell. After years with him and using a little bit of the love spells my mom taught me, he really was leaving me. He really thought it was over, but if he thought he was going to leave that easily then he had another thing coming.

"I see that look on your face, Alyssa, and I'm telling you this now, you can try some slick shit if you want to but I will not have your back. You'd be all alone," Courtney said as if she could read my thoughts.

"I'm not going to do anything crazy, damn. I just wanted the tea on the situation. You know I got my own thing going on now, anyway," I lied. I was dealing with someone when Romelo and I were in the middle of our breakup but I ended that. The truth was no one knew how to put it down in the bedroom like him. Now, Jenae was getting my man and the nigga was doing more for her than he ever did for me.

CHAPTER TEN

ROMELO

"So, when do you want to get married?" Jenae asked as she moved her dinner around on her plate. "Like in the next year or so?"

"That's all up to you," I replied.

"I don't know when I want to do it. I just know that I want to marry you. There's no doubt in my mind that."

"Then, that's all that matters," I told her making her put a smile on her face. "Why are you picking at your food though?"

"I don't know. I guess I'm not really hungry," she replied. "Did you want to get the check and do something else?"

I licked my lips because my thoughts automatically went to devouring her body. "Somebody else like what?"

"Not what your freaky ass is thinking about. I was thinking about something like a show or going to gamble."

"Whatever you want to do is what I'm going to do," I said. I wanted to go with the flow since she thought I'd tried to take over the trip when we first arrived.

"Gamble that way we can do some drinking."

I played craps while Jenae watched and got drunk. Five Pina Coladas later I had her up on my back to carry her to our room. I dropped her onto the bed and wanted to go out on the balcony so that I could call Antonio and Justin check on things in Baltimore.

"Where are you going?" Jenae asked as I was walking away.

"I gotta make a couple of phone calls."

"Okay but not before you give me some dick," she replied as she pulled down her strapless dress along with her bra, revealing her perfect breasts with her Hershey kiss nipples.

"I promise I'll be right back. But get that pussy wet for a nigga."

"Okay, Daddy," Jenae said before she stood up to take off the rest of her clothes. As soon as I saw her bare pussy, I wanted to turn around and dive in, but I needed to check on my business. I went out on the balcony and I called Antonio first but he didn't answer s I called Justin's phone.

"Yo, bro," Justin said as soon as he answered the phone.

"What's up? How the demo at the club going?" I quizzed.

"Good. I just left there with Ant and the whole bar and kitchen got taken out already. Rashad is meeting with the contractor in the morning."

"That's good. Make sure them Mexicans stay on track in there."

"I am. How's Vegas? You having fun?"

"Yeah. I was just calling to check on you but Jenae's waiting on me."

"Alright, I'm gonna keep shit on track."

"Good. I'll talk to you tomorrow, bro. By the time I ended the phone call and got back to the room, Jenae was laying on top of the covers, completely naked, but sleeping. I could've let her sleep, but I wanted some birthday sex.

I pulled her body down on the bed so that I could place her legs on my shoulder. The moment my tongue touched her clit, Jenae's head popped up and a moan escaped her lips. "Ooh, yes. Right there," she said as she held onto the top of my head.

Once I had her right where I wanted her, on the brink of an orgasm, I stood up and pulled down my pants and entered her. "You awake now?"

"Oooh, fuck yes! I'm awake," she moaned as I pounded into her. "This my pussy, right?" I asked.

"Yes, Daddy. It's all yours."

"This pretty pink pussy belongs to me?"

"Mmmm, yes," Jenae moaned as she twisted her nipples.

"You gonna cum for daddy," I said as I rubbed her clit.

Almost instantly she started raining her juices all on my dick, making it slippery and wet. I bent down and kissed her while I slowed down my pace. I didn't want to cum too soon. Our lips parted and I told Jenae to get on top. I laid back and enjoyed the show while Jenae bounced up and down on my dick.

When she shuddered and collapsed on my chest from another orgasm, I kissed her forehead and flipped her over so I could dig her back out. I held onto her sides and went as deep as I could with every stroke. Jenae was a G though. She never ran. She took it until I was coming inside of her.

I laid on her bed and she rested on my chest. "Happy Birthday, Melo."

"Thank you, love."

ERYKAH

"How long this bitch gonna be mad about a nigga that she doesn't even want?" I asked my best friend, Jabria.

"You sure she don't want him?" Jabria asked, answering my question with a question of her own.

"I don't even know at this point. I sent her a message apologizing. I know she read it but she ain't say shit back. Like, it's not that deep. Cisco for everybody and she know that. Besides, the nigga came on to me."

"You know you sound crazy, right?" Jabria said with an eyebrow raised.

"How I sound crazy?" She wasn't making any sense to me.

"Because you don't have boundaries. I'm telling you that if you did some shit like that to me, I'm fucking you up with no hesitation."

I sucked my teeth. "I doubt that."

"You got issues, Erykah."

"How the hell you gonna say I'm the one with the issues? I don't bother anybody."

"You're lucky that Sabrina didn't put her hands on you and the only reason she probably didn't was because you're her sister. You and I both know that Sabrina ain't no scary bitch and she got hands."

"Whatever," I said as I attempted to flag her with my left hand but the nail tech wasn't letting that shit go.

"Who did you go to the damn party with anyway?"

"I went with Sabrina."

"Damn. So, did you even get a good look a Melo to see if he's into Jenae like that or if it's just a rebound since he was with his old bitch for so long."

"Oh, with all the shit I was telling you about Cisco and Bree, I forgot to tell you the crazy ass news," I said knowing that once I laid the bomb that I had on her, she'd be forgetting all about my antics.

"What? Spill. You know I love me some good ass tea, especially when it's about sexy ass Melo."

By then you could practically hear a pin drop because all the ladies in there wanted to know about Romelo and his new mystery chick. "They're engaged. That nigga popped the question to her after only three fucking weeks."

"You fucking lying," Jabria said with shock

179

written all over her face.

"I'm dead ass serious right now. She living with him and everything. You should have seen the fucking car he got her for her birthday, not to mention that big ass ring. That's really a come up for her 'cause she was just working at Tracee salon shampooing hair, now she got fucking Melo taking care of her."

"How she luck up on that? She ain't even that damn cute. It's always the plain jane bitches that get these niggas. In the meantime, I'm putting my best fucking foot forward and I can't get my baby daddy to take care of his daughter, let alone some nigga to take care of me." Jabria said.

I couldn't agree with her 100% on that because Jenae was always super pretty and she took good care of herself, but I was sure that she wouldn't know what to do with a nigga like Romelo. I was sure that she wouldn't appreciate all the shit he was about to put her onto. Mike was more her speed since he was slightly above broke. I needed a nigga like Romelo, but for the time being, Cisco would have to do.

LEILANI

"Why the fuck is his baby mom calling my phone constantly and commenting under my pictures?" I asked my sister. I didn't really want to call her with my drama while she was away on vacation, but I couldn't help myself. She was getting under my skin.

"Why would she do that? I thought y'all were good," Jenae said. I couldn't tell if she was being sarcastic or serious because her voice was so even toned.

"We were," I said before I let out a melancholy sigh. "She's pregnant by Keraun. I didn't really want to say anything."

"How far along is she? Like is she due soon or something 'cause I know you said that you've been dealing with him for like six months, right?"

"She's only twelve weeks or something like that. It was before Keraun and I decided to be exclusive so he didn't cheat or anything but she was nice and now she's being a bitch to me. It's all because Keraun told her that he wasn't going to leave me alone."

"All I can say is to ignore her. Don't feed into the bullshit. Block her from calling and block her Instagram. You don't owe her anything. Let Keraun deal with her pettiness." Jenae always gave good advice but a part of me wanted to curse Paris out.

"I know but…"

"But nothing. I swear you're gonna make it worse for yourself and if she's real petty she may try to keep him from his kids. You don't want that."

I sucked my teeth because everything in me was telling me to fight fire with fire, however, Jenae had a point. I didn't want to be the cause of Keraun not being able to see his kids. "Okay. I'll make sure that I stay calm. I swear if the bitch wasn't pregnant—"

"Then you still wouldn't do anything. Every time you want to fuck her up, you have to remember that she's your man's baby mom. That'll help you save her ass."

"Alright. Oh, when will you be back. Mommy and Daddy found out about you being engaged and they want to meet Romelo as soon as possible."

"How did they find that out?" Jenae asked and I expected her to be panicked but she seemed calm as hell.

"I don't know. Tracee told her mom or something and Aunt Connie told Daddy. Well, that's what he's saying but you know Daddy got an Instagram now, so he could have found out that way."

"That old ass man don't have no Instagram," Jenae said shocked.

Our father wasn't old at all. He was only forty-five but I could see where Jenae was coming from. No one wanted their parents on Instagram. Parents already took over Facebook.

"Jamal helped him get one. Anyway, Mommy told me to tell you that you better not be pregnant and to answer her phone calls, whether you're on vacation or not."

"Ain't nobody pregnant," I said with an attitude.

"She said that she wasn't watching any more kids since Jamal baby mom keeps dropping off Rilei."

"Whatever. That's not my problem. I'm not ruining my vacation 'cause she wants to be all up in my business," I replied.

"That's our mom, though. You know how she is," I said as Keraun pulled up on me. I was standing outside of the library at my school. I wasn't expecting to see him because my best friend Jazzi was supposed to pick me up. We were supposed to go and get drinks. "I'll see you later, though. Keraun just pulled up out of nowhere."

"Alright. Stay out of trouble," Jenae said before I

hung up the phone.

I slipped my phone into my back pocket and walked up to Keraun's car. He had the driver side window rolled down. I stuck my head inside and gave him a kiss on the lips. "What are you doing here? I thought I told you that I was going out with Jazzi tonight."

"I can't check up on you?"

"Umm, not on campus. I may not have even been here. What's up?" I asked as I stood upright.

"Take a ride with me, real quick. I'll drop you off to Jazzi house afterward. Call her and tell her."

I stood with my hands on my hips. "You don't just get to make demands. I'm not flaking out on my best friend."

"Lani, just get in the car 'cause all you're 'bout to do is piss me off."

I sucked my teeth but got in the car. I had no clue where he was about to take me, but as long as it wasn't around Paris, I was good. I sent a quick text to Jazzi to let her know I was with Keraun: *Keraun kidnapped me. He promised that he'll take me to your house afterward, so we're still on for drinks.*

Less than a minute later, Jazzi was texting me back: *Seriously! I was just driving over to the library. You better not stand me up either. I have so much I need to catch you up on about my dumb ass nigga.*

Me: *What did ES do now?*

Jazzi: *Just come to my house so I can tell you. It's too much to text.*

Me: *Okay. I'll be there.*

CHAPTER ELEVEN

ROMELO

"You know what would be crazy?" Jenae asked.

I was sitting on the floor between her legs while she rubbed my temples. "What?"

"If we skipped all the wedding planning and went to a quickie wedding chapel to get married.

I turned around so that I could get a good look at her. "You sure that's something that you want to do? I ain't even meet your pops, yet. You don't want to have anything here with you?"

She shrugged. "I wasn't saying that it had to be today. I meant whenever we were ready. I don't really care about everyone else and what they have to say, though. I love you and want to spend my life with you. That's all that matters to me but if you want to wait, then that's fine too."

I stood up and said, "All right. Let's get married."

Jenae's face flashed a few emotions, first confusion, then nervousness, before it finally rested on happiness. She was smiling from ear to ear when she said, "Okay, then let's do this." She had on a pair of my Champion sweatpants and a white tank top.

"You want to change your clothes?" I quizzed.

"Why? So you can change your mind? Nope."

I laughed but grabbed the car keys and headed out the door with Jenae hot on my trail. Once we were in the car she began to Google search wedding chapels. "Which one do you prefer? We can go to the Elvis themed wedding chapel or we can go to the drive through one."

"I don't want no dead white nigga doing our wedding so let's got to the drive through."

"Okay, I'm putting that into my GPS then."

I'd never been a drive through wedding chapel in my life and didn't think that I ever would. I didn't think that I'd ever be getting married, yet there I was driving down the Las Vegas Strip heading to the Little White Wedding Chapel.

We stayed in the car the entire time and the minister had us say our vows at the same time. I looked into Jenae's eyes, while she looked into mine, all while holding her damn phone up because she wanted to record it. As soon as the dude said that he pronounced us man and wife, I pulled her in close for a kiss.

When Jenae pulled back and dropped her hands into her face. "I can't believe we just did this. I can't believe I'm married."

"Well believe it, Mrs. Moore."

"I like the sound of that. I'm Mrs. Jenae Moore."

"Now, let's go back to the room. I'm tryna fuck my wife," I said playfully.

She punched me on the arm. "You can't talk like that now that I'm your wife, babe."

SABRINA

Cisco was blowing up my phone. It seemed like I couldn't get any peace between Cisco constantly calling, Erykah throwing subliminals on Twitter, and Mike's dumb ass was still coming to my fucking apartment crying buckets of tears, looking for Jenae. Everything and everyone were getting on my nerves. On top of all of that, my manager at my store was riding my ass. I needed a break from it all. I always found solace with Justin, so that was exactly where I went.

When I got off work, I did a pop up at Justin's apartment. It was my first time doing one. I knew that he would be home because he said that he was staying in to watch the game with a few friends from college. I didn't have a key but the doorman knew me and let me right up. I knocked on the door and it was opened right up for me.

It wasn't Justin that answered the door. It was his friend, Jay. "Yo, Justin, your girl's here."

There were about four other guys in the apartment, not including Justin. I found him in the kitchen getting himself a beer.

"Hey babe," I said as soon as I reached him and gave Justin a kiss on the lips.

"What's up? You want a beer?" he asked. I nodded my head yes as he handed me an already opened bottle of Corona.

"I didn't know you were having a party," I said feeling as if I was interrupting his guy time.

"Naw, it's not a party. It's just the fellas. The game almost over though. You want to watch it with me, or you want to go to the room and lay down. You look tired."

The last thing that I wanted to hear from my man was that I looked tired. "I'm a little tired," I lied. "I'm gonna go lay down in the bed."

"Okay," Justin kissed me on the forehead. "I'll be in there to check o you when the game's over."

"Cool." I walked away and waved to the rest of Justin's friends that I hadn't spoken to when I arrived. I didn't really want to lay down but I didn't want to watch a baseball game with a bunch of frat boys either.

I laid in the bed and texted Jenae but she didn't reply, so I sent a text to Leilani and got no response, then I resigned and laid in the bed. I must have drifted off to sleep because I felt Justin kissing me on the forehead. My eyes fluttered open and I saw him standing above me. I sat up and asked, "Is the game over?"

"Yeah. It ended a while ago. I came in to check on you but you were knocked out. You hungry?"

"Yeah. I haven't had anything to eat since my lunch break. Can we go out to dinner?" I got out of bed and started putting my jeans back on.

"We can if you want to drive."

"I'll drive. I'm just starving. Can we go to Buffalo Wild Wings?"

"Buffalo Wild Wings it is then."

I didn't like driving with Justin in my car because he always complained about how slow I drove. I tried to explain to him that my grandmother taught me how to drive when she was sixty-eight, therefore I was very cautious when I drove.

Buffalo Wild Wings was crowded as hell because I failed to realize that there was a basketball game and it was the playoffs. Justin and I were having a good time. He was being a great listening ear so I vented about my manager. I didn't tell him about my feelings regarding Erykah fucking Cisco, nor did I tell him that Mike was still looking for Jenae.

"Is that Erykah?" Justin asked cutting me off mid-sentence.

I turned my head and looked in the direction that he was peering in. Sure enough, it was Erykah sitting at the bar eating wings with none other than Cisco. There was a knot in my throat and my stomach burned. I was fighting back tears because I knew Justin would flip if he saw me getting emotional at the sight of them. "Oh," I finally squeaked out. If I would have said a full sentence my emotions would have betrayed me.

"You want to go?" Justin asked.

"Yeah. I'm not speaking to Erykah and I don't want her to see me."

We hadn't gotten our check but we came to Buffalo Wild Wings enough and always ordered the same thing so he knew exactly how much the food was. Justin dropped $70 on the table, which was more than enough and we bounced. The two of us were almost home free but Erykah noticed me. "Damn, I know you see me, Bree. You not gonna speak?"

I stopped dead in my tracks and looked at her. My body was burning hot with anger. I wanted to hit her so bad but I didn't want to cause a scene and I didn't want to hit my sister. "Why would you think I'd speak if I'm not even answering your texts. I'm not about to be fake. I really don't want anything to do with you."

"Yo, Sabrina, let's go." Justin jerked my hand, jumpstarting our movement and I had to walk away without saying another word.

When the two of us were back in the car, Justin said, "I thought you let that shit go. Why are you letting her hoe ass get to you?"

I didn't respond to him because I didn't want to end up saying something I would later regret. I was in my feelings and I could have easily taken it out on Justin.

LEILANI

"When are you taking me to Jazzi's house? I thought you wanted to take a ride and talk, not go shopping and then to run around doing drop offs," I said complaining. Keraun picked me up four hours ago and it was getting late.

Keraun squeezed my thigh in an attempt to calm me down. "I'll get you to her."

"Yeah but when?" I asked because a squeeze on the thigh wasn't about to pacify me.

Keraun huffed and said, "I'm gonna drop you off now man since you don't want to hang out with your nigga."

"Thank you."

Keraun didn't say anything else to me as he drove over East towards Jazzi's house. When he pulled up, I tried to give him a kiss on the lips but he turned his head on the side. "You acting like a lil' bitch right now."

Keraun looked at me and I could see steam coming out the top of his head with how angry he was. "Who the fuck you think you talking to like that?"

"Key, you need to calm down. I only said that to get a reaction. You won't even kiss me because you're mad that I won't let you ruin my plans. How that look? Come on now."

Keraun calmed down a bit when I said that but not a lot. "You spending the night at my house tonight or you going home?"

"That depends on if you're going to pick me up when I call you," I replied.

"Have Jazzi drop you off at my house. Use the key I gave you. I might not be home when you're done."

I laughed a bit because he really was in his feelings. "Okay. I'll see you later." I didn't attempt to kiss him. I just grabbed my backpack and got out the car. I left my shopping bags because the things were just going to his house, although I wanted to show Jazzi my new Gucci bag, but I would have to wait until another time to do that.

"Don't be out here wildin' either."

"Bye, Key," I said walking up to Jazzi's house. I didn't even get to ring the bell before her door swung open. She waved at Keraun, who hadn't yet pulled off before pulling me into the house and closing the door behind her.

Jazzi lived with her mom and grandmother. All the living room furniture was straight out of the seventies and covered in plastic. No one was allowed to sit on it. There was no TV in the living room. They converted the basement into the family room and that's exactly where we went but we stopped at the liquor cabinet first and got a bottle of Ciroc.

"What the fuck took you so long? I thought you weren't ever gonna come. Girl, so much shit happened since the last time I saw you. Why you let Keraun kidnap you like that?" Jazzi talked a mile a minute. When we first met in seventh grade, I couldn't understand a word she said and no matter how many time I told her to slow down she never did.

"I didn't think he was going to take so long. I thought he wanted to talk about something important, like his damn baby mama playing on my phone but he just wanted to spend quality time. I did get a bomb ass Gucci bad out of it so I'm not too mad."

"Wait, I thought Paris liked you. What do you mean she's harassing you?"

I forgot that I didn't tell Jazzi about Paris flipping the script as far as her feelings about me. I let out a deep sigh. "Girl, it's a big thing." I poured some Ciroc over the ice in my glass.

"Is it? Tell me what happened," Jazzi lived for the tea.

"You know how I told you Keraun said that he got her pregnant. Well, he went over there to find out what happened at her last appointment because he couldn't make it and she told him that she was twelve weeks and showed him the ultrasound of the of the twins. He said that everything was normal until he mentioned that I said I wanted to speak to her. The bitch flipped wondering why he was staying with me when she was pregnant. He said that nothing that he said would calm her down. Finally, he just left and after that Paris called me.

"I answered it not knowing what had gone down between the two of them, thinking she was going to ask me to pick up the youngest from daycare for her since it's down the street from Keraun's house and neither of them could make it. I'd done it in the past so it wouldn't have ne a big deal, but nope. That's not what she wanted. This bitch started cursing me out, calling me all kinds of names and said that I was a homewrecker. I hung up and she went on Instagram and posted a whole picture of me saying all this shit.

"I tried ignoring her ass but she's been commenting on pictures and mentioning me in tweets, the whole nine. I wanted to bust her upside her head but Jenae said that it wouldn't be the best idea so I'm just biting my tongue. It's hard as hell though 'cause you know I'll fuck a bitch up."

"Awww, I'm so proud of you for keeping your composure, 'cause any other time you'd be dragging me to the girl's house," Jazzi said.

"Right! I can't though 'cause I don't want to affect Keraun's relationship with his kids."

"How did I not know all this was happening?"

"'Cause you had that damn paper due. That's all you kept talking about. I didn't see you for two weeks because of it. Did you turn it in? How did you do?"

"I turned it in and I got a B+ on it so I'm definitely not complaining. But, let me tell you about the drama," Jazzi said getting to the point of why I was visiting in the first place.

"So you know I been trying to give ES a second chance after I caught him with that bitch he flew in from Charlotte. Well, why did the bitch send me a Facebook messenger request, or whatever, and tell me that she's still fucking him," Jazzi said when I listened intently. She was always animated whenever she told me a story. She used her entire body to make sure you felt every moment of it and this was not different.

"You know I'm not about to just let some random ass bitch tell me that she's fuckin' my nigga and not have proof. Like, if you fuckin' my nigga I need receipts. This bitch like, 'If you want receipts, I screenshot all of our conversations.'"

"You fuckin' lying?"

"Nope, I'm not. She sent me everything. Took the nigga name off of the contact so I could see his damn phone number and that it was really him. I was through."

"Did you call ES about it?" I quizzed.

"Hell yeah, and the nigga lied because that's really what he does best."

"So, what are you going to do? Are you going to stay with him or are you gonna bounce? I know he puts you through a lot of shit with these damn hoes."

Jazzi shrugged before she sipped her drink. "I don't even know. I'm like, I can end things and let that hoe win or I can stay with him but if I do he's gonna think that it's cool to do whatever the fuck he wants to me and he can't. What do you think that I should do?"

"I don't know. I can't answer that for you but you deserve more than a nigga who's gonna play with your emotions and that's exactly what he's doing, right now."

"You're right but I love him and I'll miss the way he holds me when we're together. There's no way I can give that shit up."

CHAPTER TWELVE

JENAE

"Are you gonna spend the whole morning on the phone or are you about to get back in the bed with your wife?" I asked as I watched Romelo pace back and forth at the foot of the bed. I didn't know who he was on the phone with, nor did I care. It was our last full day in Las Vegas and our first full day as a married couple. I wanted his undivided attention.

He must have sensed that because he put his index finger up, indicating that he needed a moment longer to continue his conversation. I didn't want to be all up in it, therefore, I pulled out my phone and texted Sabrina and Leilani in a group text: *When I get home, have I got some news for y'all. And don't try to get me to tell you before then. See y'all tomorrow night.*

Leilani: *Wait, what?*

Sabrina: *No, bitch. You don't come in this group text and tell me you got news for us then try to bounce. You have to tell us now. It's only right.*

Me: *I can't. I promised Melo that I would wait. Just make sure that y'all can meet for drinks tomorrow night around ten.*

Sabrina: *Ugh, I guess, but I still feel some kind of way.*

Leilani: *I do too, but I'll be there. And the tea better be piping fucking hot.*

Me: *I promise, it will be.*

"You ready?" Romelo asked and I didn't realize he was off the phone.

"Ready for what? Some dick?" I asked.

"Nah. To get some breakfast, go shopping and then to the pool party you been talking about."

I forgot all about the things we had planned for the day because I was officially a newlywed and wanted to jump my husband's bones. "Okay. Let me jump in the shower. I'll be ready in like fifteen minutes."

"We both know that's a lie. I'm gonna go get some coffee, though. I'll be back."

"Okay." I hopped up out of bed, kissed Romelo on the lips and ran to the bathroom. I wanted to stick to the timeframe that I quoted him so I showered as quickly as I knew how.

I still must have taken a long time because when I stepped out the bathroom he was back with his coffee and my caramel macchiato. "Please tell me that there was no line out at the Starbucks this morning."

"Nah, babe. That line was long as hell, but at least you're out the shower. I really thought you'd still be in it when I got back." He handed me the cup.

I took a tentative sip to test how it was before I spoke. The coffee was hot but not unbearable, just the way I preferred it. "I already know what I'm wearing so it shouldn't be too long."

"You telling me you're not about to have like eight outfit changes?" Romelo joked.

"Nope. I want to wear my shorts with the new Gucci t-shirt and my Gucci flip flops. I'll change for the pool party later," I said as I put on my panties followed by my bra.

"You hype about your Gucci shit."

"I sure the hell am. I always had a few designer

pieces, but it was a Louis bag here and a Gucci bag there. I never really had clothes and I like this Gucci shirt. It's so classic," I said before I popped the tag off the shirt and pulled it over my head.

"You gonna have to get used to it, Nae."

"I'll try to but I'm not sure I ever will," I replied.

I only filled in my eyebrows and put on lip gloss before we went to breakfast. It was at breakfast that Romelo dropped a bomb on me. "You gonna keep working for Tracee?"

"Yeah. Why? You don't want me to?" I asked as I cut my waffle into little pieces.

"I prefer you don't. I plan on taking care of you, so it's not like you have to."

"I know that I don't have to but I like my job. I don't think I'll stay there forever or anything but I don't want to have nothing going on in my life."

"You've got YouTube," Romelo replied as if that was a suitable solution.

"I'm not even popping on YouTube yet. I'll probably work for Tracee until I'm making enough money from YouTube for it to really be an income."

"But you don't need an income," Romelo said looking me in the eyes. "I'm your income."

"And what if something happens to you? What if something happens between us? What do I do then?"

"Nothing's going to happen to me and nothing's going to happen between us. However, if it does, I'll always make sure you're taken care of. You don't have to doubt that." I knew that Romelo was sincere in what he was saying but there was no way I was quitting my job. I couldn't just leave my cousin hanging.

"I don't know how long I'll be working for Tracee but I'm not quitting as soon as we get back," I said.

Romelo looked like he was mulling over the idea of having a wife who worked before he finally said, "Fine but if you get pregnant, I don't want you working."

"That's fair, however, I don't plan on having any kids anytime soon. I'm staying on my birth control."

"I don't want to rush you into having kids. I want to make sure you're ready when they come along," he replied and I smiled.

During the conversation, I realized that when you rush to get married, there were a lot of things that I never asked or thought to ask. I wondered how many more things we would clash on.

"My parents found out that we got engaged and it wasn't from me so it's going to be a really big deal when they find out that we got married," I said. "My mom is cool. I'm just nervous about telling my dad."

"If you were nervous then why did you do it?"

I laughed before saying, "'Cause I'm not nervous for me. I'm nervous for you. My daddy is crazy. You'll see that soon enough."

"Crazy, like the nigga gonna get a shotgun?"

I nodded with a chuckle. "But he may not get it since I'm not pregnant. My dad is cool as hell though. He'll be shocked at first but more than likely, he'll embrace you with open arms. As long as you make me happy, he's happy."

"I promise to keep you happy for the rest of my life," Romelo said causing me to blush. It may have been fast as hell, but I truly loved that man.

ROMELO

"You like this one?" I asked Jenae while we were in the Cartier store, looking at wedding bands.

"Does it have one that matches for you?" she quizzed.

"I don't know. I don't work here," I replied.

Jenae sucked her teeth and walked off to find the girl that offered us assistance when we first walked in. I didn't realize that Jenae would have so many questions so I told her no. Now Jenae was irritated with me and I found it funny. I walked behind her and listened as she said, "Do you have any wedding bands that will match for me and my husband?"

"Oh of course," the bubbly little white girl responded. "They're right over here."

Jenae and I followed behind her to a display. Jenae looked through the glass while I stood over to the side. Whatever she picked was fine by me.

"A lot of people like the Love Rings. Were you looking for something with diamonds?" the salesgirl asked.

Jenae looked back at me. "Do you want

diamonds?"

"Nah, but you can get diamonds," I replied. I didn't need a bunch of diamonds but Jenae could get whatever she wanted.

"Umm...okay. So, he doesn't want diamonds but I do. So you can give him the plain one as long as it's platinum. For me, can I try on this small one with the diamonds?" Jenae asked.

"Sure thing," the salesgirl said as she opened the case and pulled out the rings that Jenae requested. I looked over her shoulder and I liked her selection. "Do you know what ring sizes you guys wear?"

"I wear a six and a half and he wears a size ten," Jenae said answering for the both of us.

"Great. The one that I have right here for you is a six and a half so you can try that on, but the size ten is in the back. I'll go and get that for you," the salesgirl said before she walked away. I was surprised that he was walking off, leaving Jenae with the ring but as I looked around, I noticed that there was a security guard staring at us intently.

"Do you like it?" I asked Jenae as she tried it on.

"Yeah. Do you like it? Do you think it goes well with the engagement ring?" Jenae asked me as we both looked at the ring on her finger.

"Yeah 'cause the engagement ring only got the one diamond so it's not competing with the band," I replied.

Jenae smiled before saying, "You're right. I like this."

"So you want it?" I quizzed hoping she said yes because I didn't want to spend the entire day shopping for rings.

"Yeah, it's perfect," Jenae said with a huge smile on her face.

That was all I needed to hear. When the salesgirl returned with the ring in my size, I slid it on and it fit like a glove. "We'll take these," I replied pulling out my black card. We were in the store for about fifteen minutes getting everything squared away.

I had my ring on my finger and I thought that it would bother me but I was surprised that it was a comforting feeling. It was a reminder that I'd made the decision to spend the rest of my life with Jenae and I was perfectly fine with that.

"What time is this party?" I asked Jenae.

"Soon. Do you still want to go?" she quizzed.

"Yeah if you got tickets. It may be fun. Is it gonna be black people there?" I asked her.

"Probably. I've seen pictures from parties there and it's always filled with black people," she replied. "I guess we should go back to the room to get changed. It's over at seven."

The two of us went back to the room to get dressed. I was nervous that she was going to wear that same yellow bikini she'd been wearing because I didn't want to have to fight niggas for looking at her. However, she emerged from the bathroom in a white one piece. It was cut high up on the sides but it wasn't all the way up her ass like the yellow bikini so I wasn't too upset, plus she put on a pair of black denim shorts so her ass was covered.

"You ready?" I asked.

"Yes, sir. Are we driving? It's at the Hard Rock at their pool Rehab. It the singer Brooke-Lynn's party. I didn't even realize it when I got the tickets so I'm sure that it'll be bomb as hell," Jenae said as she slid her feet into a pair of flip flops.

"That does sound like it will be good," I replied.

When we arrived at the party it was packed. Jenae got us regular admission tickets but that wasn't going to fly with me. I found someone who was able to get the two of us a cabana because there was nothing that I was going to do half-assed.

We were sitting at the table drinking while Jenae

took pictures and uploaded every moment up to Snapchat when I noticed Brooke-Lynn walking past. She was from our city and the moment that she saw me, she stopped and came inside the cabana, while her bodyguard stood right outside.

"Romelo, what are you doing here?" she asked as she came over to give me a hug.

"I'm here with my wife to celebrate our birthdays," I replied. Jenae was so into her phone that she didn't notice me talking to Brooke-Lynne.

"Your wife?" Brooke-Lynne asked surprised before the turned around to look at Jenae. "That's her?"

"Yeah. She in her own little world right now with Snapchat," I replied because Jenae still hadn't noticed that I was talking to someone.

"That's crazy. Congratulations. When did you get married?" Brooke-Lynne asked me.

The two of us grew up on the same block and went to the same high school. We were really good friends but fell out of touch after we went off to college.

I laughed a bit before I answered her. "We got married last night. It was a spur of the moment type of thing."

"That's what's up. I want to meet her, or do you think you can't pry her away from her phone?" Brooke-Lynne joked.

"Nae," I called out and Jenae finally looked up from her phone. "Come here. I want you to meet someone."

Jenae looked from me to Brooke-Lynne and a look of shock flashed on her face before she smiled brightly. "Hi."

Brooke-Lynne extended her hand for Jenae to shake it. "Nice to meet you. Me and Melo go way back."

"It's nice to meet you too," Jenae said as she tried to smooth her hair.

"Oh and congratulations on the wedding. I'm surprised that you got this one to settle down. He always said that he was never going to get married," Brooke-Lynne said and she was right.

"I guess I'm a lucky girl," Jenae said smiling.

"You really are," Brooke-Lynne looked back at me with a smile causing me to look away. "Anyway, I better get going and host this party. It was nice seeing you, Melo. Don't be a stranger. Hit me up on Instagram."

"Got you," I said as I gave Brooke-Lynne one last

hug before she walked away. I took a seat and Jenae came over and straddled me.

"You used to talk to her didn't you?" she quizzed.

"And if I did?" I said, answering her question with a question of my own.

"Nothing. I'm just curious," she said before she kissed me on the lips.

"Yeah, when we were younger, but it was really nothing," I said as I rubbed on her booty.

Jenae laughed as she kissed me.

"What's so funny?" I queried.

"I won out over Brooke-Lynne which is bomb as hell."

It was my turn to laugh. "It wasn't a competition."

"That doesn't matter."

JENAE

Romelo dropped our bags at the front door and I walked up to him to give him a kiss. "I'm going to meet up with Leilani and Sabrina. I'll see you later."

"You leaving already? I thought that you might want to chill in the house," Romelo said surprised that I was about to run right out the door after we just got home from vacation.

"Don't you have to go meet with Antoine and Justin in the next half hour? I heard you when we were in the car, that's the only reason I told them I would meet them for drinks."

"Yeah, you right," he admitted.

I walked up close to him and pressed my body up against his. "You want to stay in the house so that we can spend some *quality* time together?"

Romelo grabbed me by my ass as he tongued me down. He lifted me up and I wrapped my legs around his waist. Our lips never parted as he carried me over to the couch before he threw me down and tore my clothes off. I had a pair of lace Hanky Panky thongs and he ripped those as well before he entered me. I dropped my head back in ecstasy because I could feel the oncoming orgasm.

"Flip over," Romelo demanded once I came for the first time. I did just that and threw it back at him until he was having his own orgasm.

It was a quickie but I had to go and take a shower before I could meet with my sister and Sabrina. Therefore, it was another half hour before either of us were able to get back out the house. I went to meet up with them for drinks and tacos. I arrived at the restaurant first and got a table in the back. Leilani and Sabrina arrived together and the hostess walked them over to me.

I couldn't even say hi before Leilani said, "Tell us what it is because Sabrina and I have been coming up with a bunch of theories."

I laughed before saying, "Can y'all at least sit down before I tell you what happened?"

Sabrina sucked her teeth before she sat down. As soon as they were both in their seats our waiter approached us asking for our drink order. I ordered our usual for the three of us. "Can we have a pitcher of frozen blood orange margaritas?"

"Sure thing. I'll be right back with your chips and salsa," the waiter replied before he walked off.

"Okay, now the waiter's gone so tell me what the big news is," Sabrina urged.

I picked up my phone and pulled up the video that I took in selfie mode of my wedding to Romelo. "Here, watch this video."

Their eyes were glued to my phone screen. It was Leilani who figured it out first, exactly what she was looking at. "Bitch y'all didn't?" she quizzed looking at me.

"Yup," I said as I lifted up my left hand so they could see my wedding band that had joined my engagement ring. "I's married now."

"Oh my goodness," Sabrina screamed causing the entire restaurant to look at us.

"Congratulations. I can't believe that y'all got married," Leilani added.

I looked down at my ring and then up at the smiles on their faces. "Right! I can't believe it either, but it's true."

"What made y'all get married? Were y'all drunk?" Sabrina asked because she had no filter.

"No. I just kept thinking about trying to eventually plan a wedding when I just asked him if he wanted a big one. It was Melo that suggested we go to a wedding chapel right then and there, but we were sober."

"So what does this mean?" Leilani asked.

"What do you mean?" I was confused by her question.

"Does it mean that you're going to have kids and shit soon? Are you still going to start recording YouTube videos again?" my sister clarified.

"Oh. No, I'm not having kids anytime soon. I want to enjoy being with Romelo, do some traveling and all of that. I'm going to start posting on YouTube again since he got me the camera and computer. Not too much is going to change though. I'm just married, that's all."

"And you gotta tell your parents?" Sabrina asked.

"Yeah. Romelo and I are going to take them out to dinner to let them know," I replied.

Leilani laughed as soon as I finished my sentence. "Y'all taking them to a public place so that they'll act right? I know that's right. When are y'all going to dinner? I want to come."

"Mommy said that if you do come, you have to bring Keraun," I replied causing her to suck her teeth.

"Then I'm not coming," Leilani said.

"You don't actually have a choice in the matter. And before you try to blame me for it, no it wasn't me who thought of the idea. It was your mother."

Leilani flagged me with her hand and changed the subject. "Does Romelo's ex know that he's married now?"

"I don't know what that bitch knows and I surely don't give a fuck," I replied. Alyssa was the last thing on my hand.

"Do you think that he'll tell her?" Sabrina quizzed.

"Ummm, no. He doesn't want to have anything to do with her," I told them.

"You think that she stalks your Instagram?" Leilani asked.

I shook my head no. "I'm private so I don't know how she would be able to."

"You should make your page public. The only reason you were private was because of that girl that was messing with Mike, but that was years ago," Sabrina said urging me to open up my page.

I didn't care either way so I picked up my phone and made my page public. Almost instantly, I gained about a hundred followers because I had a bunch of follow requests that I'd ignored. "Well, I guess I'm public now, but does that mean that the people I've blocked can now see my page?" I quizzed.

"No. If you blocked them then they'll stay

blocked unless you go and unblock them, so no, Mike and that girl Maddie won't see your page," Sabrina said knowing exactly why I was nervous.

"I don't want Mike to know that I'm married yet 'cause that nigga is crazy," I said thinking back on the fact that he was still trying to get back with me.

"You know the nigga still stopping by my house?" Sabrina asked.

"What?" Leilani asked with her eyes wide. "Did you tell Justin? Better yet, Jenae, you need to get Romelo to take care of him because I don't think he'll stop until Melo checks his ass."

I shook my head from side to side. "No, I don't want any real-life beef to start because of it. Mike already thinks that Romelo and I got together because of some imaginary beef that the two of them had. Mike's wound too tight so I don't want Romelo to poke the bear. If anything, I'll have to take to him, myself."

CHAPTER THIRTEEN

ALYSSA

I was laying on the couch in Courtney's house and couldn't believe my eyes. Romelo married that bitch while they were in Las Vegas. I was happy to be alone since Courtney would have for sure told me to get over it. My heart was shattered into so many pieces that I'd never be able to count.

I was religiously stalking her Instagram page since the moment I noticed she was no longer private. She probably opened up her page just for me to see the news and get under my skin. That bitch, Jenae, knew exactly what she was doing. I had to call Romelo to see what was really up because there had to be more to the story. The shit was just beyond belief. It had to all be one big joke.

I listened as the phone rang and rang in my ear. Just when I was ready to give up and press the end button, I heard a woman say, "Hello?"

"Ummm…" I didn't know what to say in response.

"Alyssa? What did you need?" the woman asked and that's when it clicked to me that it was Jenae I was speaking to.

"Can I speak to Romelo, please?" As much as I wanted to curse her out I knew that wouldn't get me anywhere.

"You know what? I'm in a good mood and since you asked so nicely, I'll give you the phone. But… don't take that shit as a guarantee that he'll talk to you," she said before she let out a vicious laugh.

I pulled my phone away from my ear and looked at it because I couldn't believe that she was speaking to me that way. I didn't say anything else though. I just put the phone to my ear and waited to hear Romelo's baritone voice. I could hear Jenae speaking to him but not directly into the phone. "Babe, your old bitch is on the phone for you."

"Who Alyssa?" he replied and my heart began to race when I heard him speak my name. "Why the hell would you even answer for her. I don't want to speak to that hoe."

And, just like that, I was crushed, once again. Jenae didn't even have the courtesy to tell me that Romelo didn't want to speak to me, she just hung up on my ass. When I heard those three beeps that told me the call had ended, I threw my phone across the room, where it hit the floor. I knew the screen was broken and with the fact that my job at Footlocker wasn't going to pay for a new phone or even a new phone screen. I sat up on the couch and cried into my hands until Courtney walked into the house with her friend, Solana.

"Why the hell is your phone over here on the floor? Did you throw it against the wall?" Courtney asked as she picked up the phone. The moment she saw my face she said, "What happened? Why are you crying?"

"Because Romelo got married. I called him on the phone and she answered. I don't know what to do," I admitted as I tried to wipe my tears away since they were both looking at me like I was officially psycho.

"So, you broke your phone? How did you even know that they got married?" Courtney asked as she walked over to me and handed me my iPhone that now had a shattered screen.

"Jenae's Instagram page isn't private anymore so I was able to see it. They got married in Vegas," I replied as I examined my phone.

"I know. I saw her Instagram and it was on Melo's Snapchat too. But why are you crying over it? That nigga not anywhere crying over you," Courtney said and that was exactly the response I expected out of her.

"Romelo married that pretty chocolate girl that he was in the club with?" Solana asked.

"Yup, in like a drive through place when she took him to Vegas for his birthday," Courtney replied as if I wasn't sitting in the same room as her with a broken heart.

"Damn that was fast. She came out of nowhere," Solana said. "I'm happy for them though. You know I love black love."

"I only met her briefly but from what everyone has said, she's really good for him," Courtney added.

I had to remove myself from the room because it was clear that neither of them cared about how I felt. I need to find a place of my own because no matter what, Courtney was always going to be Team Romelo.

ROMELO

"We gotta take you to the fucking strip club since you ain't have a bachelor party," Antoine suggested. We were both in the barber shop. I needed a haircut before I met with Jenae's parents over dinner later that evening.

"No, I don't. I'm good. I don't need to see no strippers when I got my lady at home," I replied.

"You not about to be one of those boring ass married niggas now, are you?" my barber JC asked.

"Nah, I just don't need a bachelor party. I'm good," I replied.

"I feel you on that but I need to meet shorty. I keep hearing you talk about her. Do she got any friends or sisters for me?" JC asked.

"None for you, nigga. Her best friend is with Justin and her little sister is Keraun's new chick. Besides, every nigga in here know you ain't ever gonna chill with just one bitch," I pointed out.

"Nigga, you're fucking married so anything is possible," Antoine interjected.

"Right!" JC agreed as he and Antoine gave each

other dap for emphasis.

"Y'all niggas tripping," I said with a chuckle.

"Nah, but for real, what made you marry shorty so quick? She pregnant or something?" JC asked.

"No, we just didn't feel like we needed to wait. I'm telling you that when I used to hear my pops say that he knew my mom was the one when they met, I thought he was bullshitting. Like, ain't no bitch ever gonna walk by me and I just know I want to marry her on sight. Maybe, I'd want to fuck her on sight, but not marry her. That was until I met Jenae and she felt the same way." It was all new to me but when you find the one it completely changes your whole way of thinking. I didn't see myself with Alyssa for much longer and that didn't have anything to do with meeting Jenae. My relationship with Alyssa had died long ago. I just didn't want to end it because I didn't want to seem like the bad guy.

"Well best of luck with that, man. I hope she don't suddenly turn out to be crazy," JC joked.

"Yeah, chicks always know how to hide their crazy side until they got your ass reeled in," Antoine added.

"Nigga, you just scarred because of what

happened when you was fucking with Robyn. You know you allowed to get your car fixed, right?" I asked.

"I'm not getting it fixed 'cause I want it to be seen. I want all the people that know I was fucking with Robin to know that the trick is fucking crazy. I don't want any other nigga to fall victim to her psycho ass," Antoine tried to explain using his weird ass logic.

The entire shop laughed at that dumb shit because it really made no sense. Antoine's car was completely fucked up and it was a brand new, off the showroom floor, Yukon Denali when it got keyed and that was six months ago. You'd never catch me driving around in a fucked up car trying to prove a point. I was just about to say something else when my phone rang. It was Jenae so I answered right away. "What's up?"

"Hey, baby. Where are you?" she asked in the sweetest voice.

"I'm at the barbershop trying to get this cut. Why? You need something?"

"Yeah. I was hoping that you were home. I left my keys to the house there along with my wallet. I ran to the salon but I never attached my house keys to the new car keys and I have no money," she explained and I could hear the frustration in her voice.

"You can come to the shop and get the keys or some money, whichever you want," I replied.

"Okay. Where is the barbershop? Matter of fact, can you just text me the address?"

I sent the text and fifteen minutes later, I saw her car pulling into the open parking spot right in front of the shop. When she got out the car she had Leilani with her along with another girl I'd never seen before. The three of them walked in and before any of the niggas in the front got the wrong idea, I walked up to my wife and kissed her while grabbing her on the ass.

Jenae looked good as hell. It was like the moment I made her my wife she somehow got even more beautiful in my eyes. Her hair was freshly done and she had on a pair of jeans that hugged every curve with a black leather vest.

"You got here fast. Where were you?" I asked her.

"I was at the salon. I told you that. Can I just have some money? I don't feel like going all the way home now that I'm here. I was going to the mall with Leilani and Jazzi when I realized that I didn't have any money. The only thing I have is my ID and that's only because it was in my back pocket," she replied. "Oh, you don't know Jazzi, do you? She's Lani's best friend."

"Nah I ain't ever meet her. What's up, Jazzi?" I said giving her a wave.

"Hi," Jazzi said looking up from her phone only for a moment to speak to me.

"Nigga, you just gonna stand there? You not gonna introduce me to your wife after you just got finished telling me all about her?" JC asked.

Jenae looked over at my barber. She looked him up and down as if she were trying to figure out his angle but I took her by the hand and led her over to JC, letting her know that he was cool people.

"You right. JC, this is my wife…"

"Jenae?" JC said before I could say her name.

"If you knew who I was then why you ask him to introduce us?" Jenae asked with her hand on her hips.

I looked on as JC laughed followed by Leilani letting out a giggle. I wasn't sure what was going on and I was about to get pissed off. "I ain't know that was you at first," JC replied as he walked up on Jenae and gave her a hug before he hugged Leilani.

"Y'all know each other?" I finally asked. I was trying my hardest not to have the reaction that I wanted to. I needed to remain calm because I couldn't believe that either of them would disrespect me in such a way.

"He's my brother, Jamal's best friend. I haven't seen him in years, though," Jenae responded as she was cheesing from ear to ear.

I didn't know Jenae had a brother so it made me think that she was talking about a play brother and in my eyes, play brother meant that they slept together in the past or were still sleeping together. "You got a brother?" I asked.

"Yeah. Jamal. He's the oldest. I didn't realize that I'd never mentioned him. You'll meet him one of these days, but he lives down in Miami. I don't know when he'll be back up for a visit," Jenae said and all that red-hot anger I felt rising inside of me was extinguished. Then I realized that I knew Jamal.

"Oh shit! I know Jamal. I didn't know that was your brother," I replied.

"Yeah," Jenae said but she had a sad look on her face all of a sudden. It seemed like every day we were finding out new things about each other and I knew that it bothered her that we didn't know everything about each other yet but we had forever to learn it all.

"How much money you need though?" I asked changing the subject.

"Oh, I didn't even think about that. I don't need too much. I was really just going with Lani and Jazzi. I just don't like having zero dollars in my possession."

I reached into my pocket and handed her the knot that I had on me. I wasn't sure exactly how much it was, but I had an idea. I didn't need that much cash on me anyway. I had more in the car as well as all my credit cards. "Here, take this."

"How much is this?" Jenae asked as she examined the knot before she stuffed it in the pocket of her jacket.

"Like three," I said as I took a seat back down in the chair so JC could continue my cut.

"Three what?" Jenae asked and I had to hold in my laughter.

"Stacks. That's good?" I quizzed.

"That's more than good, Melo. I'm just going to the mall, real quick," she said. It was refreshing to hear that kind of statement coming from her even though I planned on giving her the world. If I would have given Alyssa $3000 to go to the mall with she would have considered it chump change, which is why I had to put her on a secret budget. I didn't think Alyssa was going to make me go broke but I also didn't think she deserved the world from me.

"Just take it. It's not even that much," I replied.

Jenae let out a frustrated sigh before she said, "Thank you, Melo. I'll call you later 'cause I'll need you to let me in the house."

"Okay. Be safe while you out there," I replied before she kissed me on the cheek and walked out with her little sister and friend that was stuck on mute.

ERYKAH

Sabrina finally agreed to meet with me. I'd invited her over to my house but she refused and we decided to meet at a restaurant down at the harbor. I arrived first when she came in I was sitting at the bar sipping on a glass of water. I could feel the hostility coming off of her in waves as she approached me. "So, you want to talk?"

"Yeah. Let's get a table so that we can eat," I said getting up with the glass of water in hand. I went to the hostess stand, requesting a table in the back and we were taken there straight away.

When I sat down I said, "How have you been?"

Sabrina rolled her eyes up into her head before she spoke. "You know I'm allergic to fake, Erykah. I only came out because you wouldn't stop texting me."

"What does that mean? I wasn't trying to be fake. I really wanted to know how you were doing," I replied. "I thought you came out to try to fix this."

"I don't have anything that I need to fix. I didn't fuck your ex. Look, I don't want us to be beefing. If you want to be with Cisco then that's cool. I hope he makes you happy. I just don't want to be in your life anymore because this is what you do," she said and it was breaking my heart. No one wants to hear that from their little sister, especially when I basically raised her.

"You want me out of your life because of Cisco?"

Sabrina shook her head from side to side as she answered my question. "No, I want you out of my life because of you, Erykah. I promise I won't do no petty shit to you or anything. I just can't have your negative energy around me."

"I'm the negative one?" I asked pointing at myself because what she was saying was just unbelievable to me. It seemed like a dark cloud followed Sabrina around ever since the day we decided to live on our own. She never really came to terms with the issues we had with our mother, yet she was calling me the negative one.

"Yes because you give off nothing but negative energy lately," Sabrina said raising her voice. Our waitress was headed over to our table to get out orders out of the way but the moment she heard Sabrina yelling she turned on her heels quick as hell and went to check on another table.

When Sabrina continued, she was much quieter. "How many people have you done this to? I'll wait while you count." My little sister sat back with her hands folded over her chest as she waited for me to make a mental list of people I fucked over by dealing with their exes.

I had to admit the list was pretty long. There were six girls that exited my life where the reason was completely my fault. "Okay, you're right, Sabrina, but I don't want to lose you as a sister over my dumb shit. Besides, I'm pregnant."

I expected Sabrina to be happy for me, but she laughed in my face. "Who's baby is it?"

"I don't know for sure. If could be Cisco's or it could be Chuck's. For the sake of our relationship, I'm hoping that it's Chuck's," I admitted. Chuck was a guy I was seeing casually and I really did prefer for him to be my child's father.

"You keeping it?" was Sabrina's next question.

"I don't know yet. I think I want to," I admitted.

Sabrina let out a sarcastic chuckle. "Well good luck with that and with life, but I can't do this much longer. I'm out."

"So you're not even going to get something to eat?" I asked.

"Erykah, come on now. Let's be real. You know I beat bitches up for less and the only reason I'm not putting my hands on you right now is because you're my sister. However, that's the last courtesy I'm going to give you Bye."

CHAPTER FOURTEEN

JENAE

"How much longer are you gonna take to get dressed?" Romelo asked me as I tried on my third dress of the night. Everything that I purchased at the mall earlier had already been ruled out.

"I don't know. I'm nervous, okay," I admitted. It's not every day that you tell your parents that you went and got married in Las Vegas and it wasn't a mistake."

"Okay but our reservation is for eight o'clock. I don't want to be late and give a bad first impression," he explained and I knew where he was coming from so I decided that the dress I had on would have to work. It was a simple black maxi dress with long sleeves. I turned and looked at myself in the full-length mirror and I looked good.

Romelo had on a pair of blue dress pants, a pair of Gucci loafers and a crisp white v-neck t-shirt with a grey sports jacket over it. He looked and smelled like money, with his chain draped around his neck and the Rolex on his arm. Most of all that platinum wedding he was now sporting was shining.

I did a quick job on my makeup, switched my important things from my Louis Vuitton Neverfull and put them into my brand-new Yves St. Laurant, hot pink cross body bag. "I'm ready."

Romelo looked me up and down as I did a little spin for him. I could tell from the way he was biting his lower lip that he wished we didn't have plans because I felt the same exact way. "Okay, let's go."

My mom hadn't yet seen my new car, only heard about it, so I drove. We were right on time because I was parking my car, my mom was pulling into the parking lot followed by my father. My parents were no longer together but they were still the best of friends. I parked and greeted my mom first with a hug and a kiss on the cheek. "Hey, Mommy."

"Don't be kissing all over me. I'm trying to meet this new boyfriend of yours or should I say fiancé?" my mother said as she tried to get free from my embrace.

"Dang, okay. Well, Mom, this is Romelo. Melo this is my mom," I said just as my father was approaching.

"It's nice to meet you," Romelo told her. I was shocked to see that it looked like the nigga was shy. The moment my father approached, Romelo swallowed hard as if a knot had formed in his throat. "What's up, Beetle?"

"How's it going, youngin'? If I would have known that it was you that Jenae was with, then I would have skipped this whole dinner shit," my father said catching me off guard.

"Daddy, you know Romelo?" I asked.

"Yeah. Now, let's get inside. Where is Lani at? She wasn't coming with y'all?" my father asked as we followed behind him to the restaurant.

"No, but she's on her way. She's coming with her boyfriend since Mommy said that she wanted to meet him too," I explained.

We were all seated and had already placed our drink orders before Leilani and Keraun arrived. "Sorry, we're late. I don't know how I got lost coming here," Leilani said taking her seat.

"Keraun let you drive?" I asked surprised because Leilani was one of the worst drivers on the road.

"Yeah, but you acting like I don't know how to drive though. I just took a wrong turn. I'm here now, though," she fussed.

"Okay, but you're late," I replied.

"Girls, stop it, damn," my mother jumped in because she knew that the two of us could go on bickering for hours.

"Sorry, Mom," I said.

"Did you tell them yet? Did I miss it?" Leilani asked.

"Tell us what?" my dad asked. "You pregnant, Nae? Is that why you wanted us all to come to dinner?"

"No, I'm not pregnant," I said as I looked down at my ring. "We got married in Vegas."

"Married?" my mom asked, eyes glistening with tears that were ready to drop.

"Yeah. We didn't want to wait," I said while

Romelo held onto my shaking thigh under the table.

"Then this is a fucking celebration," my father said standing up. "Waiter! Waiter!" he yelled across the restaurant embarrassing the hell out of me.

Our waiter came over as fast as he could without running. "Yes?" he looked nervous wondering why my dad was yelling like that.

"I need two bottles of your best champagne. This is a celebration tonight. My daughter just got married," my father said before he took a seat.

"Sure thing," the waiter replied and just as fast as he'd appeared he was gone.

I was embarrassed but that was my father. Beetle was larger than life and he made sure that we celebrated my marriage in a grand fashion. I wasn't sure why I was nervous to tell him about the wedding in the first place. He was happy as long as his daughters were happy and at that moment, Leilani and I were both happy.

When the check came, the bill was a little over $1100 and Beetle tried to pay, but Romelo insisted that he take care of the bill. Our parents left right away, but Leilani and I lingered in the parking lot because I had to ask her a few questions away from our parents.

"You weren't drinking tonight? Why now?" I asked as we stood by the door. There was a light drizzle so Romelo and Keraun went to get our cars and keep up from getting too wet.

"You're so damn nosey," Leilani said avoiding the question.

"Okay, but why weren't you drinking? You pregnant?" I asked.

She sucked her teeth. "Really, Nae? There could have been a plethora of reasons I wasn't drinking."

"Like what?" I asked.

"Like, maybe I didn't want to drink or maybe I'm taking medicine that I can't drink with," she replied.

"Okay, so are you on medicine?" I queried.

"No," she said almost yelling.

"Then you're pregnant, bitch," I said because I just knew I was right on the money.

Leilani sucked her teeth for the second time

during our conversation. "Yes, I'm pregnant, but I haven't told Key yet and I'm not sure if I'm keeping it. So, keep quiet, please."

I put my finger to my lips. "Your secret is safe with me."

Leilani smiled at me before we embraced each other in a hug. I felt like things were finally coming together for us and there wasn't anything that could bring us down. But that kind of happiness often times are very short lived. I just prayed that wouldn't be the case for us.

ROMELO

"Hello," I said answering Antoine's phone call. I was driving over to Jenae who was standing out in front of the restaurant. I could hear sirens blaring through the line in the background when I answered the phone so my heart was beating in my throat. I knew that whatever reason Antoine was calling, it couldn't be good. "What's going on?"

Jenae got in the car and attempted to kiss me, but when she saw the look on my face she said, "You okay?"

I put my finger up so that she could wait a second. I needed to hear what Antoine had to say. It was hard to make it out through the sirens. All I could hear was, "…on fire."

"What's on fire?" I yelled.

"The fuckin' club. Get down here," Antoine yelled in response.

I sped off. I still had my phone to my ear, but I wasn't listening to Antoine so I hung up. I needed to focus on getting there as fast as possible.

"What's going on?" Jenae asked as she put on her seatbelt.

I ignored her because I needed to focus on making it to the club without getting the two of us into an accident. Instead of asking me repeatedly what was going on, Jenae sat back as I drove.

The closer we got to the club I could see smoke billowing into the air. It was a complete inferno and the street was blocked off once we finally pulled up. My jaw dropped when I saw it. I naïvely thought it would be a tiny fire that was already being maintained by the fire department. I never thought that the entire building would be ablaze.

I found Antonio and said, "Yo, what the fuck happened?"

"I don't even know. I got a call cause somebody driving by saw that it was on fire," Antonio responded.

"Did you talk to…" I attempted to ask, but I was cut off because a cop was walking up on me.

"Are you Mr. Moore?" the cop asked.

"Yes, I am," I replied. I was trying to stay even toned because I was pissed as hell but I didn't want to take it out on him.

"This is your establishment correct?" the officer

quizzed and I nodded in response. "Do you know what may have started the fire? I was told that it was under renovation."

"I don't know what happened. I wasn't even here. I was at dinner with my wife about to head home when I got the call and rushed here," I replied.

"So, you have no idea what may have happened?" the officer quizzed again.

I was getting even more frustrated with him because I didn't like the way the questioning was going. "No! Like I fucking said, I was at dinner with my wife when I got the phone call and rushed down here. Isn't it y'all job to find out what the hell happened? I wasn't even..." I was laying into the cop when I felt Jenae rub my arm in an attempt to calm the fire that was building inside of me and she did just that. I changed my tone because I wasn't going to get anywhere with the officer if I cursed him out. "Look, I don't know what happened. I wish that I did because that's years of hard work all down the drain."

When I calmed down, the officer's line of questioning changed. "Do you know if the contractor was working there today?"

"I'm not even sure. My brothers were handling that for me but they're not here," I said but I couldn't focus on the conversation anymore as I watched the roof of the building cave in. My heart sank and it absolutely broke when I heard the officer's radio come alive. "There's a body in here."

-TO BE CONTINUED-

Thank you for reading!

I hope that this story has touched you in some way. There won't be too long of a wait for part two. If you enjoyed it or even if you want to leave feedback don't hesitate to leave a review. I read every single one and love hearing from my readers.

MORE FROM EVIE SHONTE

For the Love of a Boss 1-4

Loving My Street King: Jayla & Scrap 1-3

She's Too Young For a Savage

CONNECT WITH THE AUTHOR

Connect with Evie Shonte

Evieshonte.com

Instagram:
https://www.instagram.com/evie_shonte/

Facebook:
https://www.facebook.com/evie.shonte/

CPSIA information can be obtained
at www.ICGtesting.com
Printed in the USA
LVOW13s1447060218
565499LV00013B/1051/P